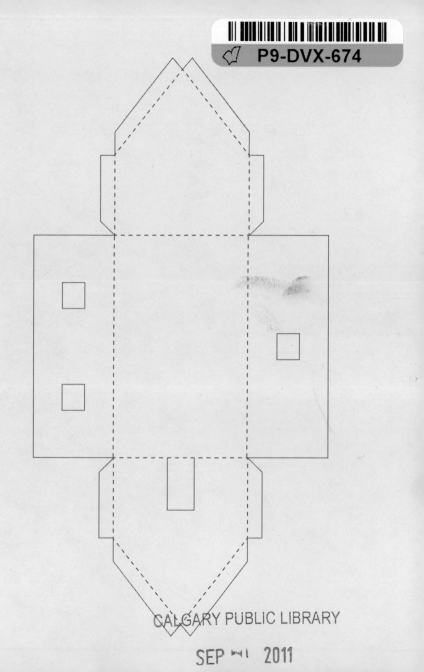

HOUSE OF SPELLS

house
of spells

A NOVEL BY

R. Pepper-Smith

NEWEST PRESS

Library and Archives Canada Cataloguing in Publication
PEPPER-SMITH, ROBERT, 1954–
HOUSE OF SPELLS / ROBERT PEPPER-SMITH.

ISBN 978-1-897126-87-5

I. TITLE.

PS8581.E634H68 2011   C813'.54   C2011-901965-5

EDITOR: THOMAS WHARTON
BOOK DESIGN: NATALIE OLSEN, KISSCUT DESIGN
AUTHOR PHOTO: ANNA ATKINSON

NEWEST PRESS ACKNOWLEDGES THE SUPPORT OF THE CANADA
COUNCIL FOR THE ARTS, THE ALBERTA FOUNDATION FOR THE
ARTS, AND THE EDMONTON ARTS COUNCIL FOR OUR PUBLISHING
PROGRAM. WE ACKNOWLEDGE THE FINANCIAL SUPPORT OF THE
GOVERNMENT OF CANADA THROUGH THE CANADA BOOK FUND
FOR OUR PUBLISHING ACTIVITIES.

201, 8540–109 STREET
EDMONTON, ALBERTA   T6G 1E6
780.432.9427
NEWEST PRESS WWW.NEWESTPRESS.COM

NO BISON WERE HARMED IN THE MAKING OF THIS BOOK.
PRINTED AND BOUND IN CANADA   1 2 3 4 5 13 12 11 10

This story is for Adrian, Kegan and Dion
and in memory of Tom Pepper.

1

I get paid to watch mountains and forests. From the fire lookout on Palliser Mountain I've memorized the peaks, the avalanche tracks, the bends in the river below, the logging roads and cut lines. When anything looks different I see it.

The tower cabin is a standard one-room with a seven-foot ceiling and four walls of four-foot-tall windows, no curtains, the chrome-legged kitchen table and chairs under the east window. My bed is under the south window and my books line the north sill. In the west corner, a sink and a small counter with a bar fridge under it, run on propane. Only the fire finder, a circular table with a topographical map and two sighting apertures, stands above the sills.

I go outside to place my pots of basil on the catwalk banister, watch clouds build over the eastern ridge, beyond the outhouse and the patch of grass the Forest Service calls a garden. Below I can see three horses at the foot of the mountain, a grey and two buckskins, the ones Mr. Giacomo lost earlier this summer.

Sometimes in that morning light an avalanche track can look like a column of smoke. Golden conifer pollen drifts over the Slocan Gorge, wisps of river fog rise off the hidden bend of the Palliser. Low clouds blow up over the eastern ridge like water flowing uphill.

Now that I'm alone, memories float in and out of my mind. I've assisted my mother at two births, one in the spring of 1969, the other this year. Mrs. Giacomo's was the first birth. Her son was born blue, couldn't be made to breathe. While my mother tried for a long time, her mouth over the baby's nose and mouth, I held Mrs. Giacomo's cold hand and she turned to the wall.

I remember the baby's puckered, bruised eyes, glued shut with a sticky film and its limp, tiny hands. Finally Mrs. Giacomo reached for her child, to take it out of my mother's arms. She could see there was no hope. She took it under the blankets next to her chest and then she drew the blanket over her head.

Even though I was only sixteen years old, I couldn't leave her there alone. I crawled under the blanket to rest my head against her shoulder, and my arms around her felt so weak and useless. She felt like she was covered in ashes. Over her shoulder I could see the face of the still one in her arms. His tiny brow looked puzzled at not entering the living world. His limp hands were delicate, hollow-boned, and the skin at his temples pale blue.

Later Mrs. Giacomo would blame my mother for the child's death. She would say that my mother had not done enough. That was the end of a long friendship.

Then this year Rose's child was born; I was there too.

My name is Lacey Wells and I've got a lot to tell you. I know who the father of Rose's baby is. His name is Michael Guzzo. He left last winter before Rose knew *she was pregnant, when the Odin Mill shut down because of the snows. He left to travel in Central America.*

I know why Mr. Giacomo wants Rose's baby and why he can't have him. And I want to make sure none of this is forgotten.

2

One night in the winter of '68, over a year before Mrs. Giacomo lost her baby, Rose wanted to see if there was ice on Olebar Lake. She liked to skate and she was waiting for the lake to skin over. She knocked at my window, and we rode bikes in the dark through falling snow to a beach that was packed with fishing huts.

We'd met the summer before, picking fruit in the Butuchi orchards. The Portuguese Alberto Braz would get us up at 5 AM, hammering at the bunkhouse door. He would drive us into the orchards in the back of his truck, the bed bumping and jarring on the potholed road with a grassy hump up the middle of it and Rose curled up and still trying to sleep, head in her arms on one side of the truck bed. He would really yell at us when we left ripe fruit in the branches that we missed or that was too hard to reach. Sometimes when he wasn't around, we played soccer on the river road, using a hard green peach for a ball.

Now we rode bikes in the dark to Olebar Lake. Onshore, Rose knelt to put her hand in the ripplets that were washing through the beach gravel. Surprised, she said the water was warm. I'd heard that there were hot springs in the lake bottom, and that sometimes, on nights like this, warm water was pushed ashore by the wind.

She went out wading, trailing her hands, the snow driving in around her.

I took off my boots and rolled up my pants to follow, the lap, lap of water that smelled of fish around my knees, groping over stones with my toes. Skin ice was splintering way out, but near the shore the lake was quivering like a mirror that had nothing to reflect. Hissing snow was drawing over it in wide curtains.

"Let's go out as far as we can," I heard Rose say, laughing. "This water is as warm as a bath. I want to dive in!"

"You'll freeze biking home," I warned her.

"I don't care. This is really wonderful!" she said, the snow collecting in a grey cap on her hair and sticking to her eyelashes.

I could hear the low chug of a barge coming across the water. A house appeared in the issuing greyness and in a gabled second-storey window I could see Mr. Giacomo peering out in lantern light as if watching the shore for drift logs. The pilot cut the engine and I could hear the rattle of the anchor chains. The house drifted quietly before us. I could see Mr. Giacomo quite clearly in the second-storey window. His father was an Italian stonemason from the valley and his mother was Japanese. Though he was in his fifties, in the lantern light his skin looked smooth and clear, like a young man's, and I liked him for it.

"Ah," Rose said, standing beside me, "that house is for Mrs. Giacomo."

The window was drawn open and he was standing there with his hands gripping the sill, looking out for a long time. The barge rocked and I could hear the crackle of the old floors and walls. Sometimes I, too, have felt that anxious need to make things better: if only this would go right for me, I might get what I want. There was no house like that in the village. He had bought it in Burton for his wife who had come from Burton. She had always dreamt of that house being hers. When she was a girl, the owner of the house, a judge, used to hold Saturday night parties for people in Burton who had money. She'd stand outside at night while the doctor, the mayor, the logging contractors and their wives passed by the uncurtained living room window in some glorious dance. Later they would settle at the brightly lit dining room table, the women smoothing out their fine dresses. I've always wanted a life like that, she'd told my mother.

When the judge died the house stood empty for a long time. There was a dispute over his will. Then it went up for sale, and Mr. Giacomo bought it with its Burton memories for his wife.

Now Rose asked the question that our village always asked: "Where does he get his money?" He told people he made his money logging in the Nachako country after the war but some people said he'd come home from occupied Japan already rich.

Though we were still and all you could hear was water rummaging along the shore, Mr. Giacomo called out, "Who's there?"

Rose gripped my hand, touched my cheek and pushed me to the beach, trailing her palms to quiet the water around her knees. Sometimes she could be like that: shy and wanting to get away before she was called out or recognized.

3

More than anyone else in the village, my mother could heal birds and other animals. Once I brought her a robin that I'd scared out of the mouth of a village cat and she set its wing. When she left to work in the canning factories of Westbank, she left the bird in the care of my father, and when she returned to find it dead, she was furious. My father told her that he'd done everything he could to keep the bird alive. He'd fed it worms from the compost and he'd placed it in a straw-lined cardboard box near the stove in his one vat paper mill and still it had died. I believe the missing ingredients were touch and voice. When my mother attended a birth, she would stroke the woman's back and belly and she would sing in a strange, low way, not really words. Mouth music she called it, sounds that entered the woman's body as the touch of palm and fingers enters the skin of a drum. You felt that whatever she was singing came from inside you, from your belly and knees.

Once when I was ten or twelve, Mr. Giacomo called out to me: "I need your mother! One of my horses is ill."

He was calling to me from an upstairs window in the Blackwater Mountain Lodge. It was spring and I was coming down from the Illecillewaet snowfield with my father's paper.

He got me to come up to the upstairs room. On a plain wooden table there was a clay bowl.

With pride in his voice, Mr. Giacomo told me the bowl was from the seventeenth century, Tokugawa period. He said that a dress spread on bamboo on the north wall was a Shikoku kimono, things he'd brought back from the war.

I'd heard that he'd bought the Blackwater Lodge and that he ran a summer trail riding camp and that he kept Savona River horses up there. In late spring and summer he took groups of girls onto the alpage, and they were often accompanied by priests from their parish.

The Blackwater Mountain Lodge was built in the twenties by Italian stonemasons from Friuli. They were hired by the railroad to repair the stone trestles in the pass. For the lodge they used shards of mountain stone, and the walls were two feet thick. In winter they used to ski there, Mr. Giacomo's father among them. After two winters he married Susan Tanabe, who came from the Yokohama prefecture in Japan. They went to Vancouver to live on Powell Street, and just before the war they returned to Japan. Mr. Giacomo, their only son, stayed behind in Vancouver. He was sixteen or seventeen then, and on his own.

The sick horse was tethered in the courtyard. "There was a storm last night," Mr. Giacomo said, "and a large oak branch fell in her corral. She ate the new leaves." He asked me to check her pulse and then to hurry down the logging spur to fetch my mother. He asked about the wooden rack I had on my back and about the paper tied to it. He smelled of new wine and lavender soap, and he began to walk the mare around in the courtyard, talking to her.

The logging spur leads from the Illecillewaet snowfields through a pine forest to the railroad tracks and then it's a two-mile walk to the village along the grade. The paper I carried weighed twenty pounds and I kept watching the weather, which was uncertain. Above me stood the Dawson Glacier across which storms came into our valley, changing the weather suddenly. My father had made paper for the internment camps in New Slocan and Bay Creek, and now he sold to the artists of Baltimore and New York. Some of his paper was snow-bleached and some of it was sun-bleached. I would carry my father's paper into the Illecillewaet snowfields, to bury it in powder snow. The light filtering through

ice crystals bleached the paper, and it acquired
a pure, enduring whiteness that made it rare and
valuable.

I liked being up there on my own. My father
would only let me wander on the gentle slopes just
above the treeline where there was no chance of an
avalanche and if the weather was bad he wouldn't
let me go up there at all. I loved standing at the
edge of the treeline, looking out over the snowfield
and listening to its stillness. I loved the weightless
feel of the snow that I heaped on the paper, the way
it sparkled and flashed in the sunlight. And it made
me feel important that I was helping my father in
that way.

⊞

Bright early morning, the western sky full of stars.
My mother and I had walked up the logging spur
to the lodge, the wind over the forest an unpacked
sail. The mare stood tethered in the courtyard
among girls from the east who were enrolled in
Mr. Giacomo's riding camp. She must be kept
walking, my mother said, and she must not lie
down. I remember climbing a stone flight to the

balcony where Mr. Giacomo sat as the girls, one by one, led a horse from the stalls. The courtyard with its flapping geese and many cats was bordered on two sides by high stone walls and on one side by horse stalls under a slate roof. Mr. Giacomo poured out a glass of cider for my mother. Below, the girls were being directed by the priest who had travelled with them from Montreal.

Mr. Giacomo poured out the cider with its sharp, frothy smell of windblown apples. I was watching the priest lift the last of the girls into her saddle. The most patient horse had been chosen for the youngest. It stood there unmoving with a drooping head, both ears alert. Last night, the riding party had slept in the attic. At breakfast I'd watched them climb one by one down a ladder into the dining room, the bread and bowls of hot chocolate set out on three long tables. Those girls didn't even look at me; I envied their chatty excitement, the way they laughed and carried on over their bowls, their privilege.

"Something big, something big," Mr. Giacomo was saying and his opened hands on the balcony table were a question. The riding party had gathered under an oak outside the courtyard, waiting for the priest. In his brown cassock he rode out among the scrub oaks.

"I've got something big planned," said Mr. Giacomo, opening his arms. "I want to plant vineyards south of the village, Italian vines." My mother looked at him with questioning eyes. They walked along the icy balcony strewn with sand that the sun never touched. He said that the weather was changing in the valley, winters were milder. It was now possible, he believed, to plant wine grapes. Did my mother know, he asked, of any land that might be available?

"I've been wanting to ask you this," he told her. "You're a midwife; you hear things that other people don't hear. Maybe you know a family that's thinking about selling its land."

"I'll ask around," she said.

She and the Giacomos were friends in those days, years before their baby died. She and Mrs. Giacomo had been friends since high school.

4

About a year after the Burton house arrived by
barge, my mother and I drove to Mrs. Giacomo's
in Mr. Giacomo's car. I was stretching out my
legs in the back, on a seat that smelled of wine lees
and green alder shavings. Big flakes were sticking

to the windshield. Mr. Giacomo had turned on the wipers. When we left our yard, the Columbia Avenue street lights had come on and I could see fresh prints that horses had left in the snow in the street. There was the Mallone café, the shades pulled. I watched the snow drift under the streetlamps and gather in the corners of the darkened café windows. Above the streetlamps and above the rooftops you could feel a cloud had come into this valley and the snow fell in silent ripples. There was hardly any wind. Mr. Giacomo told us he hadn't changed over to winter tires and now and then I could hear the summer tires slip on the icy street and the engine revved.

My mother was quiet tonight. Usually she would be chattering on about this or that. But she didn't turn around to look at me. She was holding herself still, not looking to the right or left. I couldn't hear her breath over the wash wash of the wipers. Earlier that morning she had delivered twins in the Palliser Valley. She had been up all night with Mrs. Sandez and the twins were born in the morning, one after the other, around 6 AM. She'd had only a few hours to sleep before the call came from Mrs. Giacomo.

While we were waiting at home for Mr. Giacomo
to come for us, she poured well water from a small
stone pitcher into clay cups the size of thimbles
and she said, Drink up Lacey, Mrs. Giacomo's baby
will be born tonight. I saw her hands tremble when
she packed the rubber sheets, the thermos of pepper
tea that she'd left to simmer for an hour on the
stove to make it stronger.

Sometimes when I wake up I feel unsure of
myself, too. I just look around before dawn, no
bird chatter, and the night table and the wardrobe
and the mirror in my room at home don't have
their shapes yet, and I feel their wanting, as if in
my sleep I haven't given them the smile or touch
that calms them; and I feel sometimes that things,
too, are afraid in their passing, cowering a little.

Mr. Giacomo drove into a tire-rutted yard in front
of the Burton house. Grey for want of paint, the
house that had crossed Olebar Lake on a barge now
stood on a high bluff above the Palliser River. It
was too tall for our village, with peaked brows over
the upstairs windows. A harsh light shone in the

downstairs windows, as bright as the arc lamps in the train yard.

We walked up springy planks to the front door.

Inside, my mother didn't say much about how unprepared the house was for a birth, not even when she heard the roar of the propane heaters inside the front door, glanced at the arc lamps casting sheets of light on the drying plaster walls. The water in the kitchen was a garden hose stuck through the window, the stove to heat water and to warm the pepper tea was a camp stove.

This was one of Mr. Giacomo's biggest plans — to present a fine home to his wife — and the lack of order in the hallway and in the kitchen frightened me. It made me feel tired just to look at the kitchen shelves covered with a fine plaster dust and the stacks of labelled cardboard boxes. I wanted to go home.

Bothered by the lack of preparation, my mother spoke to Mr. Giacomo in a clipped, flat voice: John, she said, when she walked into the kitchen and saw the garden hose stuck through the window and all the pots still in boxes, I need pans and hot water.

Yes, he said, I'll get those for you. You go ahead

and check on my wife. He moved boxes around
on the floor, reading their labels.

The pots and pans are in here somewhere, he
said, hurrying now. I'll find them!

When she climbed the stairs to the bedroom,
her hand gliding along the varnish-flecked banister,
I saw my mother slow and turn to me with a look
of disbelief, for the upstairs, much disused, still
smelled of mould and rat droppings and the ammo-
niate smell of squirrels' nests. She shook her head,
kept climbing to the bedroom.

I think Mrs. Giacomo was in too much pain to even
notice me; the contractions were coming on full.
Her head rested on a green cushion, a cushion from
the sofa in the hallway downstairs. She looked at
my mother, her mouth a small round O of pain and
her fingers clasped on her belly. Her eyes were the
colour of the bloom on ripe plums.

I was helping John to move in, she apologized,
in the way that people do when they feel they're
being inconvenient.

It happens, my mother said. You can't always

be exactly sure when a baby is due. She went about hooking the rubber sheet on the mattress corners. She told me to go downstairs for water and towels.

In the kitchen, Mr. Giacomo, pulling open boxes, asked me how things were going. He placed two clay bowls on a shelf above the counter.

When our baby is born we'll drink from these!

Those bowls looked as lumpy as cooking apples.

I was eager to help, and even now I wonder at how helpful I wanted to be, thumbs pressed on a pot lid as I carried steaming water up to the room, by the drying plaster walls. I wanted to show my mother that I could be useful. Still, I felt something was wrong and I kept busy in order to ignore the feeling.

My mother's voice was sharp and bitter, and I kept asking what can I do and I didn't mind when she snapped at me, I can't keep telling you, placing towels under Mrs. Giacomo's hips, her back propped with pillows, and Mr. Giacomo calling from the foot of the warped stairs, What do you need?

I went up and down those stairs to fetch towels and water, by the shadowless flare of light on the muddy-smelling walls. When I climbed the stairs for the last time, my mother called out of that hot, steamy room with its painted-shut windows, her voice calm now, and I thought to find some delightful baby that you lift in your arms to feel its struggling, wailing life.

I walked into the room and my mother turned the wrapped infant towards me. I saw it take two gasps like a trout drawn onto ice, and then it lay still in her hands. All of a sudden that room smelled of the winter lake, of the warm, lichen-coloured water that sometimes welled to shore, spreading out from the deep hot spring.

She just leaned over this baby, quiet, as if listening for some far, piping tune, her eyes wide and still, without reflection.

Later she would tell my father that she had immediately brought the baby to her mouth to breathe for it, but that was after Mrs. Giacomo had shouted at her, Do something!, to shake her out of a dream. And even then she had to think of what to do, like someone who has awoken and doesn't recognize where she is.

I don't think she even heard Mrs. Giacomo shout at her. She just stood there at the foot of the

bed with the still one in her arms, just stood there.
I could see by the bewildered look in her eyes that
she had suddenly lost all confidence in herself.
I could feel her cold grief creeping into my belly
and along my inner arms, and I clapped my hands
to startle her.

5

A lot of trains pass through our station at night. The westbound trains carry grain, coal and lumber to the seaports. The eastern trains bring freight from Asia. I remember the very first train to pass through our valley delivering Japanese cars to

Ontario. It was delayed at the station that spring and a lot of people went out to look at it.

That train carried Toyota Celicas, Nissan Skylines, and Datsun 240Zs. They were all kept unlocked. I'd never seen so many cars stacked like that before. They looked like ornaments; a trick of light had raised a metallic glow on them.

Rose and I climbed the double-decker car flats to sit behind steering wheels that smelled of vinyl and oily metal. We were really becoming friends that spring, a few months after the Giacomo baby died. She climbed quicker than I could, like a raccoon, and now and then she'd look down at me to laugh encouragingly. I could smell on the cars an odour of oil and diesel smoke. I climbed into one and sat behind the steering wheel just to pretend I was driving past the 4th Street girls at the village fountain who were tossing water at each other from cider bottles, past Bruce Hiraki who was the son of my father's friend Mr. Hiraki. He was a little in love with Amy Mallone, whose father owned the café Mr. Giacomo was to buy, and rather than kiss her, he scooped water from the fountain to toss at her. I sat there, the train at rest, and Rose called down to me,

Want to drive a Nissan Skyline? To the coast?
Want that one down there?

She climbed with ease, her arms strong from
working horses in summer. I'd seen her walk
Clydesdales down our main street, when she
brought those horses out of the forest for the fire
season. Rose's family were horse loggers on the Big
Bend where our river turns round, flowing south
instead of north. In the fall of '67 they'd sent her
to our village to attend school, and she'd stayed on
Mrs. Beruski's farm south of town. She was around
sixteen then, with those big horses walking beside
her past the Columbia Bakery. They followed her
like two obedient dogs. She was feeding them cider
apples from her pocket. Now and then one would
nuzzle her shoulder, snuffle the lank hair at the
nape of her neck.

Those horses were the size of a full-grown
moose. Their iron shoes rang out on the pavement.
She liked to look in their serene eyes then. Had
one of those animals misplaced a step, it could
have crushed her foot. Up close they seemed to
dwarf the cars parked along the sidewalk, blocked
them from view. Her family used them to haul logs

out of the forest, to the shores of Olebar Lake. She whistled to make them lift their head to look at her, then they went back to nuzzling her pocket, pushing her along so that she laughed. She was walking them to Mrs. Beruski's farm on the flats south of our village; they'd stay there till the fire season was over.

Do you want to drive to the coast, Rose was saying, in this one? She was calling down to me through the open window of the car she was in.

Not really to go to the west coast. She was already pregnant then and she needed a friend. I wasn't sure of her, maybe because I felt her need for a home where she'd feel safe, a need that I didn't know how to answer. Still, I liked her laughter that was an invitation to cross the distance between us.

Sure, I'll go to the west coast with you, I said then. You drive, I'm coming up there.

Well, come on then! and I heard her voice settle and grow more assured. Maybe it was then that she began to trust our friendship.

6

Later in the summer, Rose and I were lying on our
bellies on Michael Guzzo's raft off Olebar Beach.
Michael Guzzo was Rose's boyfriend. She'd met him
in Burton. When she described him, his unkempt
sandy hair, the green logger's vest that he always

wore, his mild, chestnut-coloured eyes, I knew who he was. Before he left to travel in the winter of '69, I'd seen him in the Grizzly Bookstore from time to time, going through the secondhand books.

We were kicking the raft through the still water at dusk. I heard voices from the picnic tables under the bone dead oaks near the point. I heard two voices — a man's and a woman's — arguing and hushing each other. Rose said, That sounds like your mother.

When Mr. Giacomo shouted, You girls must be cold out there!, I recognized his voice, and he went to the barbecue pit to build us a fire. Whoever was with him had left.

I wondered what he was doing there. It was the first time that he seemed really interested in us. I thought then that the woman he was arguing with could have been my mother, but I couldn't tell. She had stayed away from the Giacomos since their baby's death and I didn't understand what she could be doing talking with him on Olebar Beach.

Later in the fall, I'd find out why. At our kitchen table, my mother would spread adoption papers before Rose, and then I'd understand that she and

Mr. Giacomo had been planning this all summer, that they'd met on the beach to talk about the adoption of Rose's child.

Rose was at the mast and I was in the water, kicking along the raft. By then it was almost dark, though I could see the oaks on shore that had died in the winter of 1968. I told her that I'd got a summer job working relief in a fire tower and that I'd be gone maybe weeks at a time. She looked at me then, and I saw sadness draw into her eyes, as if she'd miss me. I was surprised at how she felt; we'd only been friends for a few months. She turned on a flashlight secured to the mast with duct tape. The beam swept the beach, picking out Mr. Giacomo sitting on a drift log.

Rose, don't shine people, I said, embarrassed.

Well, at least I'm not flashing him, she replied.

We dragged the raft onto the gravel and went to sit by the fire, shivering in towels. We had stayed out on the water too long, and because the lake was rimmed by mountains on the western side, darkness had fallen suddenly.

Girls, it's too dark to bike home, Mr. Giacomo said. I'll give you a ride.

He owned the only taxi in our village, and he'd driven to the beach in that car. We loaded our bikes into the trunk. The whole time Rose was laughing, because to fit two bikes into the taxi was like trying to cram nine feet of trellis wire into a tin can: jumble of handlebars, pedals in spokes, hands blackened with grease and road dust, a smear on Rose's cheek.

She had never actually met Mr. Giacomo before.

She was laughing out of shyness and not wanting to look at him.

Amused, he stood watching us. When the bikes were in the trunk he cinched down the lid with rope. The pouches under his eyes looked bruised and his strong hands that worked the rope were as small as Rose's.

I'd known the Giacomos for years.

His wife and my mother had been friends since high school. My father had worked with Mr. Giacomo when he was a young man, delivering mail to the internment camp in New Slocan during the Second World War. He and my father bought vegetables grown in the camp to sell in our village.

At his feet were a small grey satchel and a sketch pad. He took some papers out of the satchel to show to Rose. Then he looked at her, seemed to change his mind, and put them away.

⊞

The car that he drove us home in, this "Johnny's Taxi," a 1964 Chevrolet, used to belong to my mother. One summer she'd worked in the canning factories of Westbank to make the money to buy it, and then she went for her driver's license.

It turned out that she was afraid to drive that old boat of a car: the pedals confused her and sometimes she stepped on the gas when she meant to brake, the car surging, and she'd pull over to the shoulder gravel in a sweat.

And then there weren't a lot of births in the valley, so she couldn't afford gas or repairs. She got the Italian truck farmers to pick her up when their wives were in labour. In the spring of 1967 she sold that black Chevrolet to Mr. Giacomo, and he made it into "Johnny's Taxi," the letters stenciled in white paint on the front door panels. This was just one of his moneymaking ideas. He owned vineyards and orchards south of our village; for a while, he was even a trail guide with horses.

Rose, shivering in the back seat, her shirttails wet and stuck to her swimsuit, a striped terrycloth towel draped over her knees and bunched under her so that she wouldn't wet the vinyl seat, asked who Johnny was.

"Johnny," he told her, was his first name: John Giacomo.

We looked at each other and laughed: he was no Johnny. Just as the village called the priest "Father," so they called Mr. Giacomo "Mr. Giacomo." It was just the way people talked about him. He did all kinds of jobs and dressed like any working man. Looking at him you'd think he was poor, but we all knew he was rich.

We drove through the Palliser Valley past the Italian truck farms, past Mr. Pradolini's house and Mrs. Hiraki's house, both two-storey clapboard wwii houses that had been moved up from Renata after the dam was built:

Down there, nobody bothered with curtains, so you could see deep into kitchens and living rooms and the barns were wide open, lit up, with someone bedding down the cows, and I saw Mrs. Hiraki look up from her kitchen table at the car

on the gravel road; she came to the window to
watch us go by.

She looked out in a peering, alarmed way, as if
our lights meant an accident or a death. I saw her
raise a hand to shield the kitchen glare so she could
see through. Now on her own, she came from a valley
family that had been here since before the war. Her
husband had died of a heart attack, after he retired
from the Odin Mill, and her son Bruce Hiraki had
recently died in a logging accident south of the Big
Bend. He was felling a cedar when a root-rotted fir
on the edge of the clearcut tumbled and caught him
on the side of the head. I remembered my mother
telling me about the accident. News travelled quickly
in our village. I remembered seeing him toss water
at girls at the village fountain, the way he looked
at Amy Mallone with a merry glint in his eye. And
I felt a stillness settle in me then, a deep ache in
my chest.

I was there when the tree hit him, Mr. Giacomo
told us. I helped lay him out in the truck bed and
we took him to the hospital in Naramata, but it was
already too late. He was bleeding from the ears and
he'd already stopped breathing. We had to drive for

miles along the reservoir before we could turn west below the dam, towards the hospital.

Mr. Giacomo was quiet for a while. Then he said, That dam was built ten years ago. Before it was built, in winter we'd get a week of twenty or thirty below. Six feet of snow fell. Now the weather has changed, he said, because of the reservoir behind the dam. You can even plant grape vines here.

I thought to myself then, I've never seen that dam. I've heard that it flooded the entire Renata valley, now a lake. Though I have never seen it, I dream of that water sometimes, pressing down on a drowned forest and I'm swimming over stripped trees that have lost their needles and that peer up at you like miles of ghosts.

These were all dirt farms we were going by, and the car lit up corn or sweet potatoes, or a tororo field, a quarter-acre vineyard, the nets furled and bunched on an overhead wire. You could smell manured soil and the sweet, heavy scent of grape flowers that, early for that time of year, spread through the valley on still evenings.

He told us he was the one to start wine growing in our valley and where once there had been alder copses, scrub land, and apple orchards there were now vineyards. He had even gone to Italy to buy Veneto vines that would grow on the village slopes and produce grapes that would ripen here in autumn. Over the years he'd bought up over fifty acres south of our village.

Whenever he'd come by our 4th Street house or my father's paper mill, not often over the past years, he never said hello to me. Once when I was standing right in front of him — was I eleven then? — holding out a roll of paper that he'd just bought from my father, he took it out of my hands and gazed right through me.

Now he was looking at me in the rear-view mirror, studying me, and I felt a little afraid of him. I sensed he wanted something from Rose, and maybe he had already begun to suspect I might get in the way.

As we drove along, he explained that he was re-decorating the downtown café he'd just bought from Mr. Mallone with things he'd picked up on Shido Island during the war and that he was bringing in ash wood tables and chairs that would need to be varnished. Afterwards there would be regular work, serving.

You girls have finished high school, he said. Do you want to work for me?

What will you call it, Rose asked, Johnny's Café?, and in her high spirits, in her not having to pedal home in the dark, she burst out laughing.

He didn't turn round to look at her. He kept himself still, maybe listening to her laughter. Rose, wiping the tears from her eyes, was suddenly quiet. She looked at me and shrugged, though I was sure she felt the change in him too, and it confused her, made her unsure.

After his stories and his offer, he was quiet. Maybe he was hurt by her laughter or maybe he was just amused; I couldn't tell by the expression in his eyes when he glanced at me in the mirror.

We drove into the village past the roundhouse, the doors flung open and spilling out light. We stopped in front of Mr. Giacomo's house on 4th Street. On his porch, he showed us a 30 power telescope and a drawing board lit up by a battery-powered reading lamp. He told us that he was sketching the basaltic areas south of Vieta and the Imbrium Sea on the moon, difficult because of the way the light passed quickly over the Crisium Plains.

He had to sketch quickly, he said, because the moon kept slipping out of the telescope's viewing area.

Ten degrees of brightness for the peak of Aristarchus, he said, the highest degree of brightness on the moon. It could only be expressed by the purest white paper. Five degrees for the walls of Argo, expressed by slight shading. He drew on paper my father made; it got whiter as it aged.

Rose smiled at the drawing he showed us, her teeth chattering.

You girls are cold, Mr. Giacomo said then. You'd better go home and change.

When we had closed his gate behind us, Rose turned and said,

Thank you for the ride!

He called out to her, Pioneer E is going to pass by the moon on its way to the sun tonight, and take photos of the face of the moon we never see!

Who cares, Rose said under her breath, and she glanced at me in a way that made me laugh.

I turned round to see if Mr. Giacomo had heard. He'd given us a ride home, offered us work in his café. He had been kind to us. Yet I also felt

that what Rose had said was her way of keeping
to herself. Maybe even then she sensed that his
kindness had a cost.

⊞

On the walk home, pushing her bike and shivering
in her wet towel, Rose told me how she'd met
Michael Guzzo. He was working in the Odin Mill
in the fall of '69, and she used to bring lunches to
the scaler Mr. Beruski on night shift, when she was
living at Mrs. Beruski's. It was one of her duties
for reduced room and board, to take those lunches
to Mr. Beruski who measured the logs as they came
into the mill, calculating board feet. The scaler
would thank her as he unpacked his hot meal,
gnocchi sometimes, or a chicken wing pasta with
a flask of diluted wine.

Michael Guzzo was a sandy-haired eighteen-
year-old boy who drew lumber on the chain and he
wore doeskin gloves that were too big and loose on
his hands. The cedar they were cutting raised welts
on his arms, so the scaler had called to say bring
some salve along with my lunch. It was a night shift
in November and the snow she walked through had

changed to fine powder, heaped on the stacks of logs that reached to the river and collected in the chain link fence that surrounded the mill. The crew was gathered around the wood stove in the scaler's shack, under a forty-watt bulb, and this boy was at the table, his sleeves rolled back. The scaler took his flask and the metal canister of warm pasta. The others in the green chain crew smiled at Rose, standing around the stove. Their wool jackets steamed and smelled of cedar, machine oil, and the winter cold.

And when she brought out the salve from her pocket they said, From your hands, Rose, challenging her, a smile in their eyes, gentle or mocking.

She sat across from the boy, poured some salve into her hand to warm and spread on his enflamed forearms, but her hands were cold! So, elbows propped on the table, he cupped her hands in his and gently blew on them, eyes laughing at her. His eyes reminded her of her father's, so mild and chestnut-coloured. Two shy people who couldn't talk to each other. He wasn't even a year older. He wasn't particularly cute: his hair was long, sticking out from under a toque, his eyes reddened by the cold, and when he stood to rebutton his sleeves to go back to work, she saw that he was thin and a little taller than she.

He had built the raft that we'd kicked along off Olebar Beach. On weekends he used it to fish for landlocked salmon with a hand net.

I knew who he was. I often saw him in the Grizzly Bookstore, rummaging through boxes of books that people had left or forgotten on the trains. Once he said to me there is no other bookstore like it in the valley, because of those train books that came from so far away and from lives so unlike our own: *Anna Karenina, Cannery Row,* and Spinoza.

Sometimes he'd hold a book just for the weight of it, for the feel of it, as though, if he were sufficiently still and watchful, it could communicate to him its own life. And sometimes he sat there for a long time in a disused chair in the back, an unopened book in his hands. He seemed sad then and little inclined to talk. Once he held out to me the collected dialogues of Plato; the paper in that book was like a Bible's, tissue-thin and almost transparent.

There, too, you could find treasures, clothing abandoned or left on the trains. He showed me a rack of such castoffs in the back.

Who owned these things, he asked me then, smiling. Doesn't it make you wonder?

He asked me if I wanted to try on any of those clothes — a pair of jeans that looked like they would fit me, a paper raincoat from Japan, a plaid scarf, a siwash vest that was almost in style — but I shook my head. I could see a sadness in his eyes that I didn't understand.

I asked where he was from because he wasn't from our village.

He said he was from south of here.

South? I asked. Where?

Nowhere in particular, he said. My family's land is under the Hydro reservoir.

I touched his arm, shocked.

Jesus! I said.

He laughed. What can you do about it? he said. They took our houses, our land, gave us some money and told us to move on, go live somewhere else. And there's nothing we could do about it.

I felt sick, the colour draining from my face. I didn't know what to say.

Maybe that's what I feared most: to have the place where I was cared for and loved taken from me. It made me feel dizzy to think about it. If our village were wiped out, who would I even be?

It's not your worry he said, smiling and gazing at me.

All I could do was look at him.

Then he said, The dreams are the worst. Sometimes I wake up at night with a crushing weight on my chest, I can hardly breathe. It feels like the weight of all that water.

7

A few weeks later, I went to my father's one vat
paper mill. I didn't often go there because he didn't
like to be disturbed when he was working. That
day he wanted to show me a windsock made for
a newborn. I touched the painted eyes of the trout

on it. It was made to swim in the wind on a long pole and he said it was for Rose's child. He had learned to make windsocks at the internment camp in New Slocan. That was during the war, when Mr. Hiraki taught him to make paper. Mr. Hiraki and others had raised flying fish and paper horses over the camp on long poles.

"They remind us this won't last forever," Mr. Hiraki had told my father, watching the figures in the wind over the rows and rows of wooden shacks. "They give us courage."

I felt shy around my father when he was making paper; the work required his total attention. Yet I wanted to ask how he knew Rose was pregnant.

He said she swayed on her hips as though wading in a strong current, gripping her way over stones with her toes. Besides, he'd noticed her thick wrists and the loose clothes she wore.

Did I know who the father was, he asked me.

I was surprised at his curiosity. It wasn't like him to ask about other people's secrets, though in some ways our house was the clearing house for village secrets and stories. My mother was often away in other people's homes, there for grief or joy, birth or death. People often dropped by my father's mill to review their problems. His work was seen to be either odd or useless and therefore worthy of interruption. Sometimes, when he heard a truck or a car drive up, he'd go out the back door to sit among the river poplars and wait till the driver left so he could get on with his work, fretting over the thought that the paper in the press was spoiling.

Did I know who the father was, he asked me again. I shook my head, though Rose had told me his name.

I wasn't sure how much Rose wanted me to tell others then. I felt like I should protect her secret. On the raft she'd told me the father's name, Michael Guzzo. On the walk home from Mr. Giacomo's, she told me how she'd met him and that he'd gone traveling in Central America.

I was watching my father make washi paper. He was sprinkling harmica petals into the pulp, a pale mauve that was my favourite colour and that reminded me of the shadows under Mr. Giacomo's eyes and at the corners of his lips.

"What?" he was saying, he thought he'd heard me say something, but I'd said nothing, my mouth pressed into my rough sleeve and my gaze following him. I kept still because I was remembering a story I'd heard from several different people. Around here it's hard for an interesting secret to stay secret, and I've thought of it many times.

One summer in the '40s, my father and Mr. Giacomo worked together. In those days, a young man starting out on his own, Mr. Giacomo delivered mail in the valley. He took rice, letters, and packages to the Japanese internment camp in New Slocan. My father went with him, to buy vegetables and eggs in the camp that he sold to the railroad cooks.

Mr. Hiraki was interned down there. He was my father's friend from before the war. They'd worked on a section crew together, repairing track in the Odin pass, and when Mr. Hiraki had earned enough he'd bought a small farm in the valley south of our village. My father used to drive down to his farm in summer to buy vegetables.

Mr. Hiraki grows the best vegetables in the valley, he used to say, and soon he was taking orders from the village wives and the railroad cooks.

After the Pearl Harbor attack in December 1941,

all Japanese-Canadians were identified as enemy
aliens. Mr. Hiraki spoke out against the forced
evacuation of Japanese-Canadians from the coast.
Many times he said to anyone in our village streets
who would listen that the war was against Japan,
not Japanese-Canadians. "And what about you
Italians," he'd ask the Pradolinis, the Staglianos.
"Why are you not being arrested? It's because of
the colour of your skin!"

He and his family were sent to the New Slocan
camp. Before the RCMP came for them, the Hirakis
asked their Canadian friends to store household
goods. They thought they'd be back on their veg-
etable farm within a few months, that the forced
internment was only brief. My father was a young
man then and he was building his first house on
4th Street. They didn't ask one Canadian family to
take all their belongings, they asked three or four.
My father hadn't finished the second floor, so they
asked him to take the piano and a big record player.

One day my father went to look for his friend
in the camp. He found Mr. Hiraki doing what
he always did, hoeing soil to receive rain and to
trouble the roots of young weeds that he pulled

by hand. The garden earth smelled musty, like an empty chocolate box and it had flecks of eggshell in it. Under dark, shiny leaves my father could see the bulge of beetroots and under feathery leaves carrot tops the colour of the lichen you sometimes see on the north side of cedar trees. He saw that Mr. Hiraki loved every plant, every little tree, and he gave them tender care. Still, something was wrong, something in the way his friend moved from row to row said he was afraid of being singled out and attacked.

Mr. Hiraki gathered sacks of beets and potatoes, carrots and lettuce for my father. Then he raised a trout on a barbless hook from his well. It was as black as charred wood and its eyes had skinned over from a lack of light.

"The fish tells me the water is still pure," the farmer said. Then he let it down on a rope tied to a bucket, the trout circling and nosing the sides. It lived on insects that fell into the well and it was healthy and strong.

Mr. Hiraki said that he expected the well would be poisoned by people who attacked at night; he stayed awake at night, listening.

When they went into the shack for tea, Mr. Hiraki spoke of ripped-up camp gardens, of young fruit trees snapped at the trunk or torn up and laid on the ground with their roots exposed as if by a windstorm.

"Do you know who is doing this?" my father asked.

"People from the village," he replied. "They drive away before we can get to them, teenagers mostly. I've recognized a few."

"But it doesn't stop there," he went on. "The government sends us moth-infested rice. The shipment of seed potatoes that arrived last week was full of rot."

The shack that his family shared with the Kitagawas was divided into living sections without walls: a kitchen, two sleeping areas, a small altar in the main room. Lumber was expensive in the war years, so there were no inner walls.

He wouldn't accept money for the vegetables.

"What do you want, then?"

"Mulberry bark," he said. "So that we can make strong paper."

He explained that the paper would be used to

make screens to divide the shack into smaller rooms for privacy; here the two bedrooms, he said, there the kitchen.

"Paper walls," my father said, intrigued.

"If you're interested," Mr. Hiraki said, "I'll show you how."

On the drive back to the village Mr. Giacomo left the camp mail sack in the back of the truck. They went through a rainstorm and when my father insisted they pull over to bring in the sack, Mr. Giacomo drove on. He said there was no room in the cab for the sack. "Besides, everything they write is censored, torn up, misplaced, forgotten."

My father shouted at him to pull over. Mr. Giacomo looked at him, surprised, and drove on. "No one deserves to hear from them," he said.

When they got to the village, the mail was a sodden mess, a pulp of cheap tissue paper and glue.

Later that summer, Mr. Giacomo went off to a war that the Japanese were about to lose. Because his mother was Japanese-Canadian and he knew the language, he was taken to Shido Island off Korea. High-ranking prisoners of war were kept there. He interrogated officers of the Imperial Fleet, a captured prince of the imperial family. He was told to ask about artifacts and bullion that the Japanese had stolen during their occupation of Asia and their retreat.

Mr. Giacomo was proud of what he had done on Shido Island for the war effort, and he often spoke about it.

My father stayed behind. He was too young to go to war.

Instead, he learned to make paper from Mr. Hiraki almost by chance.

He delivered a truckload of mulberry branches to the New Slocan camp and stayed on to help Mr. Hiraki cut the branches to length, steam them in a steamer made out of an old dairy tank. He was ashamed of how his friend was being treated, forced off his farm to live in a shack.

My father learned to peel the green and black bark from the white bark, as if he were peeling a stick-on label off a bottle.

He scraped away bits of clinging bark with a knife.

He washed the white bark in the Lemon River, to free loose specks of black bark, and in the New Slocan camp he hung the strands to dry.

By then, the Custodian of Enemy Alien Property was selling off the inmates' belongings for a song.

The inmates made records of their possessions. They wrote on the new paper called washi that Mr. Hiraki made. It was so tough you could hide it in the well. They wrote letters to Canadian friends, instructing them to sell a fishing boat or a house on paper that could not be pulped in the rain. These letters had to be delivered by hand; any mail sent through the post office was censored, and the sale of unconfiscated property was illegal.

Now, after asking about Rose, my father was making paper that he knew I loved. With no decoration, it could be cut and folded into greeting cards. The harmica petals, stuck in the fibres, were an attraction, and the cards I made from the paper sold well in the Giacomo café. I was watching the petals fall from his sifting hand onto the deckle, pale rose colour of the Illecillewaet snowfields last evening, light that I'd seen torn into a spreading grey that vanished.

To concentrate, he kept his back to me as the sheet formed in the deckle over the vat.

He was watching the pulp settle on the bamboo screen and now I could see what the petals had made, a leaning girl with her arms out. He could feel my stillness, my gaze, and he heard me stir and get to my feet and say, "I'll bring the lanterns in for you." He didn't turn to see me go, waiting for the fibres to bind. One slight tremble of his dear hand would send out a wave that would thicken the fibres at one end and ruin the sheet.

When I returned with the lanterns, I could tell he liked this one; he was smiling over the sheet.

The swirl of petals made me think of Rose, one arm a gentle curve for balance as if she were leaning to place a glass on the floor. I remembered how she used to walk her family's Clydesdales down our main street, the reins draped loosely over her arm, a lightness in her step.

All of a sudden I felt that the figure in the paper showed me who she was.

That's *you*, Rose, I would have said to her, if she'd been there with us.

Some thin flicker of light to touch down, a lightness of spirit, tentative and apologetic. Later on, when events began to wear her away, to bear her down and push her to earth, when I'd need the courage to help her, I'd remember that figure in the paper.

Now my father was lifting the bamboo screen from the sheet draped on the post. I could smell snow in the air that had drifted in when I went outside, not that it was much warmer in the mill, too warm and the paper would spoil. He rubbed his hands in warm water on the stove; his fingers, thin and arthritic, ached so at night that sometimes he drank grappa to sleep.

"Why doesn't Rose go back to the Big Bend," he asked me then, "to stay with her parents?"

"She has no friends up there," I said. "And her mom's mad at her for getting pregnant."

He shook the water off his hands, dried them on a towel by the sink.

"We'll have to help her, then," he said.

8

Today I got out the homemade ladder and caulked the eavestroughs in a few places, hammered a few nails in the frost-heaved catwalk. A storm was building over the eastern ridge, and I tracked a harrier working its way above the pines. Harriers are pale grey long-tailed hawks with black-tipped wings. Usually they keep to the valley grasslands. They hunt rats and mice by quartering the ground, buoyant and tilting to clear the Palliser Valley fences.

Warm southwest winds climbing the ridge met colder winds from the glacier and I watched as clouds were born. Out of clear air, mare's tails appeared and rose into the mass above them. When it began to rain and sleet, I went inside to build a fire in the woodstove with chunks of subalpine fir and pine that lit like paper.

Outside, the trees bent over, the rain came in torrents, sheets that swept through the trees like hundreds of ghosts marching north.

What happens when you begin to lie to yourself?, I say to my ghosts. My mother remembers helping the young one to breathe. Yet I saw her paralyzed by grief and indecision. So it is not events themselves that make us, or what we remember of them. It's what we choose to forget, what we just can't stand to remember, that leads us by the hand down a road we can't recognize.

It would be so easy just to give up, to not try to fathom what I was beginning to feel. Last night I dreamt of the old judge's house. I felt that someone unseen had taken my hand, to lead me through its many rooms. In the dining room, a meal had been laid out on a big table lined with chairs. In another room men and women were dancing, all the furniture pushed to the walls. There was an aliveness to the house that came from the fullness of its memories. It felt cared for, and its memories reached out to hold up those dancing men and women, to give them the space of their laughter and desire.

When I awoke, I remembered how good I'd felt in that dream house, so welcomed. That feeling seemed to promise so much: that Mr. Giacomo would really help my friend Rose; that the Giacomos would overcome their grief and find the acceptance they wanted in our village.

And then I remembered how the house now stood, grey with neglect, in a bladed clearing with scarred fir roots sticking out of the earth. I remembered how it smelled of mildew and squirrels' nests. I felt then that Mr. Giacomo's kindness would have a terrible cost.

7 AM, the sawmill whistle blows. They are cutting yew, you can smell it. It smells like wet cinnamon. Through the fire tower binoculars I watch geese rise through the heavy mist on the river, lifting off the sandbar. The clouds above the village are heavy with rain.

I don't eat much. I don't like to cook and there's no-where to go out. You could make a pie or jam out of the *huckleberries on the east slope of the Slocan Gorge, and sometimes I walk down to eat a handful for something to do. Huckleberries taste bitter and sweet at the same time and they have tough skins. This morning a flock of bushtits flitted in the bushes, eating them; cheeky, they scolded me when I got close and made me laugh.*

Some days there doesn't seem to be a clear distinction between myself and the cabin and the cedars, especially the birds. I feel well when this place is in bloom and they are chattering in the bushes. Because there is never any hurry, because I can take my time, even the raggy towel I use to dry the dishes has become something like a living thing.

Sometimes I feel people are like those dappled shadows you find under a summer peach or apricot tree, growing steadily and then fading as the light fades, say when a cloud passes over the sky. Then they grow bright again and they fade, not all at once, in their own time and when they show strong light they share their warmth and when they dim they're afraid and often alone and there is no pattern to it and no ultimate reason.

9

At the end of the summer, Rose and I went into the village bar to phone about a room; she needed a place to stay for the winter when her baby would be born. Mr. Giacomo was sitting alone in one of the booths and he turned to watch us come in.

Rose led him into the talk of his loss, her eyes shining and serene.

"The baby was a tiny thing," he said, weighed almost nothing in his hands. He had made the coffin, spent an afternoon in his workshop finishing something that was no bigger than a wooden shoe-box, with a cross that he'd carved in the ash wood lid. He worked the lid with some fine chisels he'd found on Shido Island, tempered and old, wanting the afternoon alone in his grief and in his fear of what might come next. "A blow close to home — to the heart," he said, "for us to lose a child like that." He was wearing fingerless gloves and he was gazing at his hands wrapped around a coffee cup that smelled strongly of grappa, his face worn and drawn.

For the first time, Rose really looked at him. I had never seen her look so caring before. She'd overcome her shyness, which she usually expressed through laughter. It was unusual for her to be so quiet, and you never knew when she might turn what she heard into a joke, even a man's grief. Maybe because she was going to be a mother herself, she looked touched by his story.

She led him on in her quietness; he could have been talking to a mirror the way she looked at him, composed and quiet and touched his hand to listen. I wasn't sure of her friendship then; sometimes when she talked with Ian Beruski or Danny Moyer, older boys, there was a sparkling brightness in her voice, and she laughed quickly and eagerly at their jokes, when she wanted them to like her.

She brought Mr. Giacomo a plate of almonds from the bar. He hadn't eaten since morning, up in the vineyards pulling leaves to expose the fruit to the weak sun, and he was drinking grappa and coffee to warm up, he said. In his café there would be food all day but here the kitchen didn't open till five. When he looked at me his eyes were full of grief. He drained the cup, placed the taxi keys on the table. Rose helped him to his feet.

"Where do you want to go?" she asked him.

He said, "You girls drive anywhere you want." He walked like he was wading in thigh-deep water and Rose supported his arm.

"We'll go down to Mrs. Hiraki's, then, to look at a room she has for me."

She looked at me and smiled.

I wouldn't touch him. He smelled of coffee and grappa, and I was afraid that if I touched him he would fall over or crumple. Rose had trouble guiding his steps. She warned him about the raised threshold, worn oak. She had the patient voice of a nurse. When we were outside, he couldn't button his sheepskin coat. She buttoned it for him.

"This is a marvelous day," he said, sniffing at the air, eyes shining. "You girls drive anywhere you want," and he stretched out in the back seat. He rolled down a window. To clear his head, he said.

Rose drove down main street, past the Giacomo café and the swept granite steps of the town hall. "I don't have a license," she announced and we looked at each other and laughed. We left town, went under some roadside willows in a hollow by a cattle pond, trees that were always the last to put out their leaves in spring and the last to lose them in the fall, and I could smell sap where an early frost had pried into the bark. Some Charlois were standing at a pasture fence, their dark eyes turned to the taxi and behind them a field of meadow grass that reached to the foothills.

"What will you girls do," he said from the back seat, "now that the summer is over?"

I could hear him sit up, pull at his coat, his voice thick and gravelly. And I wondered, how do you get to talk like that, deliberate or knowing, I'm hardly confident in anything I say. I heard him ask what kind of place Rose was staying in, and already in his asking there was some kind of promise.

"You're staying in a summer trailer?" he asked. "There's no heat in Michael Guzzo's trailer on the Palliser. There's no phone for when that baby of yours is due, no way to call." And the promise in his tone was, Oh now, we'll find something else for you soon enough.

I was surprised he knew Rose was pregnant and so was she; she looked at me with widened eyes then shrugged. The curiosity of our village was always on the alert, and now we knew that talk had been going around about her.

I thought about Mr. Giacomo's offering to help her find a place. Oh we'll help you find something soon enough, I murmured, trying to feel the weight of his words, find the feeling behind them.

Rose drove in a startled manner, pulling the wheel to the right or left as if she felt we were drifting to the gravel shoulder or the yellow centre line.

It felt like she didn't trust her sense of distance. I'd seen her knock glasses and café spoons to the floor, reaching for them. Oh, she would cry in frustration, looking at the shattered glass on the café floor, why won't things stand! She walked like a dancer, all of her weight carried in the small of her back, but when she sat at the small linoleum table in her cramped trailer, she bumped the centre pole with her knee, spilling things.

"This is way too far down in the valley," she kept saying. "I can't live this far down!"

"You don't want to live way down here all by yourself," Mr. Giacomo agreed from the back seat. "You need to be close to the village and the hospital."

She was looking at the farmhouses and the orchards with increasing worry, as if the farther we drove the more the fields and the vineyards she didn't know made her feel alone and vulnerable.

I could have told her that Mrs. Hiraki's was miles out of town, but I didn't know that it would worry her so.

In summer we often bought vegetables and eggs at Mrs. Hiraki's farm. She would talk about the problems she was having, blighted tomatoes or rats in the pea crop. During our visits she talked just to keep us there a little longer, and she would show my father rows of withered leaves blackened with mould.

"She's lonely by herself," my father told me once, driving back to the village. "And she's having trouble managing."

Mrs. Hiraki was standing at the kitchen window when we drove into the yard, peering out. Rose parked under an old apple tree that had water wands rising out of its unpruned branches like the tines of a hayfork. Mr. Giacomo stayed behind in the taxi. "You girls go on in," he said. "I'm comfortable here. I'll just be in the way."

"They sell strong grappa in the village bar," he went on. "If I get out of this taxi now, you'll have to do my walking for me."

Mrs. Hiraki met us at the door. She took up Rose's hands and patted them between hers. She led us upstairs, glancing at Rose with a wary look, a tremor in her lips.

She showed Rose a room at the north end of the house under a sloped roof that made it feel small and cramped. She had washed the walls so that they gleamed and smelled of Lysol; under the single window there was an unpainted wooden table with a vase of dried flowers. The mattress creaked when Rose sat on it, on an iron frame that looked like it might have come from an internment shack in New Slocan. There was a porcelain basin where Rose could wash her hands and a tall wardrobe in one corner that just fit under the ceiling.

"Thank you!" Rose said. "Thank you for showing me this room." She gave me a quick, frightened look.

"There's more space here than in the trailer," she admitted.

Still, she couldn't stay. Later she said a smell of cooking came through the floor grate, the kitchen was directly below. A lot of food smells made her sick in the morning. She hated the smell of miso soup and Mrs. Hiraki had been heating miso soup.

We went downstairs, stood in the doorway to say goodbye. Rose couldn't say no to the old woman's staring, pleading look. You could tell that she hoped Rose would stay on, to help her with the farm, to keep her company. All Rose could say was, "I'll call you tomorrow."

The wind was picking up on Olebar Road when we drove home.

"When I find a place, will you help me to move?" she asked me. I knew she was only talking about a few boxes of clothes and books and some kitchen utensils.

"*We* will help you," I heard Mr. Giacomo say from the back seat. "My wife and I will help you get settled." I felt that he was testing her, to see what her reaction would be, to see how much help she would accept. Something in his voice worried me, something I couldn't make out then.

"Maybe you could move into Mrs. Camozzi's on 2nd Street," I said. Mrs. Camozzi's house had been built for the Stagliano family and now there was a sign in the window that said EIGHT BEDROOMS, and some trainmen stayed there, but maybe she didn't board girls. The hotel on Columbia Avenue was a two-storey brick building with a veranda that ran all the way around it. Road crews used to stay there, but now the rooms were rented out to old people mostly.

Why don't you come and live with us Rose, I wanted to ask her, to give her an alternative to the Giacomo's offer. We had two bedrooms, a small kitchen, and a mudroom in the back, a tiny living room that we called the parlour in a place on 4th Street people called the miner's cottage. Sometimes my father talked of building an addition but he never got around to it.

In her fear of being alone that winter, Rose did most of the talking on the drive home and mostly about herself. Her hands on the wheel looked as delicate as a child's, the skin under the nails a pale blue. Once, she leaned to peer through the windshield at apple bins at the side of the road, surprised to see them so late in the season.

Mr. Giacomo said the apples in those bins wouldn't ripen, that they were culls for the cider factory in Westbank and the jam factory in Sandon.

"I'll help you find a place," I said, turning to her. "When I'm in town I'll look after your baby for free when you get a job."

Mr. Giacomo said he could see the last of the fruit in the orchards, apples that the pickers had missed in filling their sacks to move on rather than climb for the one or two out of reach. His voice was gravelly, sleepy. It felt like he was talking just to stay awake.

"Gleaners stay into October before going to Burton," Rose said, "to cull what's left. They stay in a drafty bunkhouse where you have to light a fire at night to keep warm, burn vine cuttings or peach wood."

I could tell that she was avoiding asking for his help and that he was waiting, quiet, letting his offer settle in with all this small talk about apples.

"I don't want to live downtown," Rose said then. "I want a small place, with a sunny kitchen and a bath. I want a yard where I can plant a few flowers and grow some stuff. I want to make my own baby food and I want a porch where I can sit outside with him in the summer and nurse him without people looking. I want a plain wooden bed, not some old iron thing. And I want to be able to open the windows so the rooms smell fresh."

Her trailer had thin metal walls and an un-insulated floor. It had a propane heater under cupboards she'd painted red, but already that fall she could feel the chill of the floor through her slippers. The bed was the tabletop with the centre pole taken out and the top fixed between the bench seats so that it was like sleeping on a train bed, with your legs drawn in so that you could fit by the metal wall near your knees.

The trailer she lived in was too small for a girl with a baby. Where would she put the crib?

I couldn't tell whether Mr. Giacomo in the back seat was asleep or listening.

Now, driving back to town, I realized she was close to panic. I didn't realize that not knowing where you're going to live, that the prospect of a room like Mrs. Hiraki's could scare a person so. An early snow was falling through the streetlights and the tires creaked down Columbia Avenue, making the sound of your hand in wet hair after a shampoo. Flakes swirled over the taxi. Rose's hand darted out to snatch one from the air, to lick it from one of the wool mitts she'd put on because her hands were cold. She said that the mitt tasted of soap. There was hardly any traffic and all the store windows were dimmed. I could see tracks that horses had made and the fishtail track of a log that someone had towed to the Cowan St. Mill.

Mr. Giacomo was asleep. That night it felt like

we could take him anywhere or even leave him in
the back seat and maybe he'd awake, startled or
afraid of where he was. Nothing more I could do,
not even a blanket to cover him with. He looked
so small there, curled up and asleep, his hands
pressed between his knees.

"Where are we going to leave Mr. Giacomo?"
Rose asked.

She was driving cautiously down Columbia
Avenue, turned up 4th Street, unsure of what to
do. She left the car running in the street outside his
house, hammered on the door, and when she heard
approaching footsteps, ran laughing toward me,
saying, "Let's go!"

10

"You're working too hard," my father said. "Relax."
   "Bend your knees and back. Get into a rhythm."
   I was holding the two mould handles attached
to the deckle; I scooped some milky water from the
vat to send a wave across the mould that jumped
off the far side.

"Let me show you." He was only using his fingertips to hold the handles. "Let the rigging carry the weight. If you lift it and force it, you'll be exhausted in four sheets."

I gritted my teeth and tried and tried but I couldn't make the even waves or splashes.

I'd spent all morning watching him, the relaxed rolling of the stock across the bamboo mesh in the paper mould, arms, legs and back bent, body bouncing and nodding with the mould and splashing stock.

"Be loose. Be gentle. You have to roll and work with the bounce. Stop forcing it." I laughed. He was using the voice of Mr. Hiraki to instruct me, bits of paper fibre on his apron, in his black hair, on the window over the vat.

When I watched him, there was never a pause or a dead moment in the forming of a sheet.

Every fall my father drives about three hours from here to an abandoned goat farm in the Illecillewaet Valley, to bring out truckloads of mulberry branches. Someone had tried to grow mulberries in there, to feed to goats. He steams the branches, to strip the white inner bark that he pins under large stones behind a weir in the Palliser River, strands as long as a girl's hair. From a truckload he gets twenty pounds of bark that he makes into paper so precious that it's sold in the art markets of New York and Montreal, to watercolour artists and printmakers. His paper has almost no smell and it has the sheen of new snow.

After the paper-making lesson, I went with him to help draw that bark out of the river.

We took it into the Illecillewaet snowfields for snow bleaching. The snowfields were retreating. When I was younger, I could walk to them. Now we drove.

We spread the bark in thin layers on the snow, covering it with snow. Every day for several days we'd drive up there to turn the bark over.

He looked the fibre over carefully for flecks of black bark. Sound carried far up there and from way below I could hear the scree of a merlin hunting in the pines. Above us in the bright light the sky was almost black in the saddle between two peaks.

I loved watching my father then. The fibre was new and held many possibilities. Who knew what kind of sheets it would make? It was healthy and

strong and slowly bleaching in the snow and he
handled the fibres carefully, spreading them over
his palm as he turned them.

"Why is your mother spending so much time
with Rose?" he asked me.

"She's thinking about giving up her baby to
the Giacomos."

"The fool," he said. "She doesn't know what
she's doing."

He gently stroked the fibres as if they were
a cat's fur, turning them in the brilliant light.

"I want you to think about everything you've
known. Has it ever been good to separate a family?
Ever?"

He laid the fibres out in light so strong that
it hurt my eyes and covered them with a layer of
powder snow that sparkled and glowed, scooping
it with his bare hands.

He refused to work with gloves.

Once I asked him why and he said because the
strands were like new skin—they needed to be
touched, caressed, to make them receptive, sensitive.
In this way, he said, the paper will acquire stability,
coherence.

"Do you like Mr. Giacomo?"

He looked up at me, surprised.

"Your mother and Mrs. Giacomo have been friends since they were girls. We get along okay."

"But do you like him?"

"It's not that I don't like him, hon. I don't trust him. He was a poor man when he left for the war, scratching up a living delivering mail and selling vegetables, just like me. Then after the war he came back rich.

"I don't know how. It just doesn't make sense to me."

"He says he made his money logging in the Nachako country after the war."

"That doesn't feel right to me. I've worked with him, remember? He's always dabbling in things, never quite making a go of it. A man like that doesn't make a fortune overnight. And now he wants to dabble in being a father."

"What about your friend Rose?" he asked me then. "What are you going to do for her?"

I felt a flash of anger. "Why is that up to me?"

"You're right," he said. "Hon, it's not up to you."

"We're in a very bad place," he murmured to

himself, absently spreading handfuls of snow over the fibres. "Your mother thinks she can repair the damage done to the Giacomos, though that baby's death wasn't her fault! I don't think anyone could have saved their child."

"We'll help Rose," he said then, "when the time comes. I'm just not sure how yet."

Still, I felt angry. Maybe I was being selfish, but I wanted to ask, What about me? Who was I supposed to please? You can't please everyone when you're put in the middle between people you love. When they're tugging at you from various directions.

11

When I was four, before the dam was built, we lived
in a grey board and batten house on the Palliser
River. The aquarium was in the back room, lit by
a 100-watt bulb with a black lacquer shade over it.
I remember lifting the lid and emptying a jar into it:

crayfish, legs and pincers spread, drifted to the pea gravel. The water smelled of lichen. Here and there on the bottom were pot scrubbers of woven plastic where the young crayfish hid. It was a 20-gallon aquarium. The bottom was littered with potshard hideouts and in the middle a broken concrete block for the female with eggs on her belly. My father showed me the female's eggs by lifting it and turning it over. The crayfish's tail and legs were thrashing. Her young were used to catch winter trout.

I went with my father to catch crayfish in the Palliser, an empty mason jar tucked under my arm. His fingernails, whitish, were very thick and domed. His hands, so long in the water, showed the pale colour of winter fish. Already ice laced the shallows. He was flipping over river stones and cowling his hand to trap crayfish that were as long as my thumb, almost transparent, with pepper grain eyes and trout-coloured pincers.

"You're too small to fish on your own!" he warned me. Even at that age I had a reputation for going off on my own to catch trout. He had never seen such a child for fishing, my father told me, quick, darting hands in the Palliser shallows, flipping stones. I used to trap minnows in a nylon stocking I'd taken from my mother's drawer, laid out lines on the lake bottom. I walked out on the thin ice near the stream mouth, tapping my gumboots and calling, "Fish, fish, I'm on your ice roof!"

I had a lot of confidence then, when I was younger.

Alberto Braz had told me that the fishing was best at night. You took out a flashlight and a jar of crayfish, the hand line wrapped on a yew wood reel and you shone a light into a hole chopped in ice. The rim ice, holding black, oily water, glows from the inside and the water at the side makes lace crystals the colour of ash.

All this I was told and wanted to try.

Calling from shore, my father got me to walk into the bay, then follow the point to the fishing huts where the ice was firm.

He weighed too much to come out after me.

Sometimes I've been afraid like that, too. One winter when I was eight or nine my mother was very sick. She'd worked herself to exhaustion and caught pneumonia, was so weak that she couldn't get out of bed. Even when I went to change the sheets, she could hardly move. And when I sat there listening to her watery breath — she was asleep — I was afraid that I would discourage her, so I went to the bathroom mirror to stare the fear out of my eyes, to practice a look of composed silence and hope. When I returned, my face a cheerful mask, the sheets tangled around her legs and chest were soaked through and smelled like cold toast. She'd drawn her head back on the pillow to breathe, her throat a pale white, a hank of wet hair plastered to her ear.

She opened her eyes then, and she must have seen the look on my face.

"Don't worry, hon, I'll get better. I am getting better. You don't have to pretend everything's okay."

It was the strangest thing: I felt the mask that was my face crumple and I heard a sob in my throat.

"I don't know how to take care of you."

"But you *are* helping me, hon. You are."

12

About a week after the trip to the snowfields,
in the middle of the afternoon, I found Rose in
our kitchen. I'd been down in the yard outside
my father's one vat mill, spreading paper on yew
boards to dry in the sun.

You've made the right decision, I heard my mother say.

Rose was sitting at the kitchen table and I saw her nod. Then she turned to me and smiled and I saw panic in her eyes.

Are you sure this is the right thing? I heard her ask and I heard my mother who was standing over the stove making tea say, Yes dear, I'm sure.

There were papers spread out on the table, by a small grey satchel. That satchel was the one Mr. Giacomo had at his feet when he'd helped us pack our bikes into the trunk of Johnny's taxi, back in early summer.

What are those? I asked.

Adoption papers, Rose said.

I understood then that all summer my mother and Mr. Giacomo had been arranging this, planning this.

I sat beside Rose and she took my hand. Hers was sweaty.

You sure? I asked her.

Of course she's sure, my mother said, and she gave me a look meant to silence me. The Giacomos are a fine couple. I've known them for years. They can afford to raise and educate a child.

She brought Rose a pen and then she went quickly about making tea at the counter, not looking at Rose, as if her signing or not signing was a small, everyday matter. She wanted to make the thing seem quiet and small, because Rose looked like she was ready to bolt.

I watched Rose bite her lip, pick up the pen, and sign her name. She wrote out her name slowly, her face distracted, as if she were waiting inside herself for some sign.

Well, that was easy, she said.

How do you feel, I asked her.

Relieved.

That's right, said my mother, gathering up the papers. The last thing you need at your young age is a baby.

But Rose didn't look relieved at all. She was looking around the kitchen as if she couldn't believe where she was, as if she were looking for someone — or something — to tell her what her own heart wanted. All her lightness and confidence had left her; I could see her eyes welling with tears, which she quickly wiped away.

Well, that's that, she said, smiling bravely at me.

I have to head off now. Mr. Giacomo wants to talk to me about working in his café.

I'll come with you, Rose, I said. I could feel pressure building in my chest like an expanding balloon. My hand in hers had gone cold.

No, no, she said. I need to be by myself for a bit. And then she left.

⊞

That evening, I was helping my mother peel carrots for supper. She had been quiet since Rose left, thoughtful. I was surprised when she asked me to help with the dinner. Usually she liked to cook on her own.

When Rose was born, she told me, she was a small baby with these bright black eyes like a thrush's. I brought her home that night wrapped in a towel because her mother was exhausted and needed to sleep. I put her in your crib beside you.

Her voice was soft, distant, as she gathered up the carrot peelings from the counter.

Rose's will be my last birth, she told me. I can't go on like this. I don't have any confidence left.

It wasn't your fault that the Giacomo baby died, I said. Nobody could have saved it.

When I think about what happened, my heart freezes, she said. My hands still shake! I feel that if I'd only acted more quickly, I could have saved that baby.

This really is best for Rose, she went on. She's too young to raise a child. She's still just a girl, with a girl's future ahead of her. She can't grow up overnight. It will spoil her life.

13

One rainy afternoon in the fall, my mother brought
Rose into our house. Out in the street, in her winter
coat, Rose had felt a rush of warm fluid. She sat
beside me for a minute at the kitchen table to touch
her inner thigh. Her eyes were so still that I could

see the reflection of the kitchen window five feet away.

She unfolded a list of names that she showed me. I noticed that Michael's name wasn't in the list of boys' names. In our village, sometimes the son was named after the father. Michael had been away since last winter. At first there were a few letters that she couldn't answer because he was always on the move, then nothing. She had stopped talking about him.

"I'm not really going to keep it," she said, "but it was fun to choose names for something to do."

My mother got Rose to stand and began to help her undress, saying, "And now here you are, so young!" She helped her into a loose nightgown.

As the contractions deepened, her face crossed by brief waves of pain, Rose took my hand.

I saw that my mother's lips were drained of colour when she placed a jar of almond oil in a pan of warm water on the stove.

Her cloth bag was by the kitchen door and her birthing shoes and that loose cotton apron that she always wore that said MODERN BAKERY.

"You're in pain," my mother said.

"A little."

She led Rose to the bed, to spread almond oil on her belly. Smooth as lake water! my mother said as she massaged the oil in, her trembling thumbs pressing and rounding.

"You remind me of when I was young." She smiled. "You learn to sit on your hands, delivering babies. You learn patience."

I was sent for tea and when I returned she and my mother were laughing over the names Rose had chosen from the village telephone book. Still, there was a tension between them. Rose looked scared, unsure, and the glances she gave my mother were full of doubt. She must have felt my mother's trembling hands on her belly, their lack of confidence.

My mother was spreading a rubber sheet on the mattress, her face quiet and determined.

"I'm setting up the mattress," I heard her say to herself, "then I'll get the towels and pans of hot water," as if she were talking herself through the steps of a birth. Step by step, so that she wouldn't forget anything important.

When my mother said it was time to lie down, Rose shook her head impatiently, walking the room with her hands on her belly. When I brought her a wet cloth for her dry lips, she dropped it to the floor in a sudden wildness that made me think she'd run, vanish.

My mother took a firm grip on her hands and said, "You can't run from this. You'll only hurt yourself and the baby. Try to relax, be gentle with yourself. Breathe."

Even when her contractions were less than two minutes apart, my mother could not get her to lie down. Rose gave birth squatting over blankets heaped on the floor, holding onto the back of a chair. I held her from behind, pressing my knees into her lower back when she asked me to, my arms under hers and wrapped around her chest. I was so scared for her; I felt my own breath high in my chest, almost a sob.

"Here we go," my mother said, crouched beside Rose. "I can see the head." I could feel Rose pushing, her belly tight, and the baby slipped out. My mother caught it, held it up before us, a skinny body smeared with white mucous, a crumpled face with a pushed-in nose, two fists no bigger than my thumbs waving in the air.

With shaking hands, I put the infant in a towel after my mother had suctioned its mouth and nose and cut the cord with scissors. I gave him to Rose, who had climbed into the bed. My mother massaged her belly, to help with the afterbirth.

"You've done so well," my mother said. "So well." I saw flashes of relief in her eyes. She straightened out the pillows behind Rose's head, brushed a strand of hair from her forehead. For a moment, tenderly, she placed her palm on Rose's brow.

With one hand Rose held the baby across her chest. She lifted one of its tiny legs.

"He's a boy," she announced. My mother covered his chest and legs with a towel.

Her hand slipped to the sheets beside her, curled and listless. I put my hand into hers. It felt damp and cold. Though I was composed and still, my heart was racing.

My mother leaned over Rose, lifting the wad of cotton between her thighs. For a moment, before the blood welled, I could see marbled fat under the torn skin. My mother threaded a needle and then drew up an injection of anesthetic.

She told Rose, "His head was a bit too big for

you." Rose smiled at me with a defeated look that I'd never seen on her before.

I felt then that she was drifting away from me, far away, and that I'd failed her somehow. Her defeated look asked, Can't you help me? but I didn't know what to do.

There are two telephones in our house: one in the bedroom on the nightstand by my parent's bed where Rose held her child, one in the kitchen. My mother went into the kitchen to call Mr. Giacomo, closing the bedroom door behind her.

Rose kissed her baby.

"It's like kissing a stranger," she said. He was just staring at her. She moved her head around and he followed her with his eyes.

She closed hers. Her lips were pale with shadows underneath them. Her breath quietened and her hand gripped mine suddenly, then relaxed. The baby on her chest wrinkled his lips, curled his toes that were sticking out from under the towel.

"Don't fall asleep, Rose," I whispered. "Let's get out of here," a cold grief that I didn't understand pooling in my belly. I wanted to carry her away from there, the two of them.

My mother returned with towels, a bowl of warm water, and a handheld scale to weigh the baby. When she laid him out on a towel to wash him, he started screaming. After she'd toweled him dry, she asked Rose, "Do you want to hold him again?"

She put the baby in Rose's arms and he stopped crying right away. I didn't know that a baby could recognize its mother just by smelling her, just by knowing it's her and no one else. I hadn't been to many births, just two.

Rose unwrapped the towel to count his fingers and toes. She checked his ears, the shape of his head. He was normal, looked normal.

"He's cute," she said. "Don't you think?"

I nodded, touched his little fingers that curled warm and surprisingly strong around mine.

⊞

We heard the front door close, the clatter of boots in the foyer. Mr. Giacomo was outside in the kitchen. My mother went out to greet him.

She brought him in, and he made a point of not getting too close. He waited till my mother asked

if he wanted to hold the baby and he nodded, went
to sit in the rocking chair by the window.

It looked like he couldn't quite believe what
he had in his arms. I could tell he'd never held
a baby before. My mother had to show him how
to nestle its head in the crook of his elbow, and
it just stared up at him, wide-eyed and quiet.

"It's okay," he said. "I'll look after you."

"You'll have a good life with us," he went on,
looking down at the baby. "You'll see the house
I've bought for us."

Your window is on the south side. You can see
the river from there. We're planting a lawn where
you can play.

"My wife wants to meet you. She doesn't believe
you're real yet, and she's waiting to greet you."

Sure she wasn't there; she didn't want to see
my mom.

He was talking as if the rest of us were not in
the room, as if we'd already left.

My mother was gathering up the stained blankets from the floor, lingering there. She kept her
back to Rose and Mr. Giacomo, listening but not
turning round so I could see her face. I wanted to

clap my hands to turn her around. I wanted to know how she felt.

I squeezed Rose's hand hard to make her do something.

Rose watched Mr. Giacomo for about another minute. He didn't once look at her. He was smiling at the baby.

"You'll like your life with us," he said. "You'll have a good life."

"Will I get to see him?" Rose asked.

He didn't answer. Even then, he kept looking at the baby, but he looked startled by her question, as if it had never occurred to him.

Rose sat up. "I'm about to lose everything I've always wanted. That just hit me."

"I'm sorry," she said. "I didn't know I'd feel this way."

She drew back the blankets, wincing. In her nightdress she turned on her bottom, swinging her legs over the floor. Before she could stand up, my mother put her hands on her shoulders, saying, "Lie down. You'll tear your stitches."

"No!" Rose shouted, shrugging off my mother's hands.

She got out of bed and stood in front of Mr. Giacomo. "Okay, give him back."

Mr. Giacomo looked up at her, his eyes full of amazement. But she wouldn't go away, she just stood there in front of him.

After a minute, his face as pale as a whitewashed wall, Mr. Giacomo gave her the baby.

"I'll let you rest," he said. He touched the corners of his eyes; he looked bewildered, almost ashamed.

My father called then, to ask how Rose was doing. I picked up the phone by the bedside as soon as I heard it ring. I heard him say, "Congratulations!" Then he asked to speak to my mother and she went out into the kitchen, to pick up the other phone.

"You hang up when you hear me on the line," she said; and Mr. Giacomo followed her out.

I sensed she didn't want me or Rose to hear what she had to say to my father; her lips were tight and she had that determined look she always wore when she anticipated an argument.

⊞

Late the next night, Rose came into my room to wake me up.

"Are you going to help me pack?" she asked me. "It's time to go."

"Yes," I nodded, rubbing the sleep from my eyes.

"Hurry," she said, a false cheeriness in her voice. "I don't want to be out there in the kitchen by myself."

"I'll get dressed," and climbed out of bed.

"You're my friend, right?"

"Yes I am, Rose," I said. "I'll be there in a second."

In the kitchen, Rose showed me the bag she'd packed with dried peaches, provolone, and a cold omelet wrapped in butcher paper. "Train food is expensive," she told me, widening her eyes. She walked slowly back and forth, the click of fastened suitcase locks.

My mother got me to sit cross-legged on a chair and she laid the baby across my lap.

"That's Mr. Giacomo at the door," she said, and she went out.

The baby's breath smelled like watermelon.

What's this in my lap? His eyes followed my finger: Hey, little fellow. It felt like he was waiting for me to do something, quiet. Maybe take him out and show him the village, introduce him to folks. He had the curious look of someone who wants to

be shown around. Sometimes hikers climb to my
cabin, amazed to find it here, amazed to find a girl
so young living alone. I invite them in. I feel cauti-
ous, but the Forest Service expects me to welcome
visitors. They touch the fire finder, finger the lace
ruffle on my pillow case, touch the washed plate by
the sink, touch my little row of books on the south
sill, turn to look at all the landscape through the
wide windows. And often they say nothing, then
they thank me and they go.

I watched Rose spread the snowsuit my mother had
found for her on the chrome-legged table. The metal
zipper that she opened made the sound of an angry
hummingbird. There was a sack for the newborn's
legs and a hood of two pink ears.

In the bedroom, before she fell asleep for the
second time, we'd talked about where she was going.
She was going to Field, the next stop on the train
into the mountains, and she thought she might find
work there. A cousin who worked in the hotel up
there had said he'd help her out.

"What if you don't like it in Field?" I'd asked.

"We're not going to *stay* there," she smiled.

"We'll come back when it's okay to come back."

Now she opened her blouse, the child's greedy, wrinkled mouth at her dark nipple. "It's time to go," she said, but she still sat there as if listening, her blouse open.

Mr. Giacomo came into the kitchen. He looked away when he saw Rose breast-feeding. He asked whether the baby was healthy, and my mother, who had followed him in, nodded.

"I can do nothing more," she said, gazing at him.

He gave her a scared, little smile, as if to say, "Once again you've failed us."

And he said, looking at my mother and then at Rose, "Well, thank you for everything you've done."

Yet I could see him ask himself, What mistakes have *I* made, that have led me here? The crinkles at his eyes had deepened and paled with shame.

My father had walked up from the one vat mill. I could hear him kicking snow off his boots in the foyer.

When he came into the kitchen, rubbing his hands that were inflamed from the cold water in the pulp vat, Mr. Giacomo turned to go.

"On your way then, John?" my father asked.

"Yes," he nodded.

"Come to say goodbye?"

"Yes," he nodded again.

"How's that house of yours coming along, the one down by the river?"

"I haven't been there in awhile."

"Not here to change Rose's mind, I hope?"

My father went over to the kitchen sink to run warm water over his hands, his shoulders tight with anger. "You're not a man to respect other people's needs," he said then.

Mr. Giacomo looked puzzled, almost frightened. "I don't know what you're talking about."

"Look," he went on, "I'm only here to help. You don't have a car to take Rose to the station. Take the taxi," laying the keys on the table. "I can walk home from here."

"Thank you," he said to Rose again. "Thank you for considering our offer." He bowed slightly to her and then he turned and walked out of the kitchen without looking at my parents.

⊞

When we left the yard in Johnny's taxi, the Columbia Avenue streetlights had come on. There was the Giacomo café, the shades pulled. I watched the snow drift under the streetlamps and gather in the corners of the darkened avenue windows. Rose was quiet. Usually she would be chatting on about this or that. She didn't turn round to look at me. She was holding herself still with the newborn in her lap, not looking to the right or left, absorbed by the street ahead.

My father called this taxi "the boat."

"I'm taking you to the train in a boat!" he said. He didn't want to say, "I'm taking you to the train in Johnny's taxi." I could feel he didn't want to acknowledge a debt to Mr. Giacomo, however small.

That 1964 Chevrolet convertible felt like a river scow, solid and slow. Now my father was turning up 2nd Street towards the tracks, taking the hill in a wide arc, hands climbing on the wheel as he leaned to the left to make the car more stable.

We passed by high-peaked houses with darkened verandas. I knew who lived in those 2nd Street houses, in every one. The Camozzis and the Sandezs, the Staglianos and the one-armed yard worker Danny

Ote. I knew their lives, their memories; I'd known them for as long as I could remember. I felt held by those memories, held where I belonged. In our village, I knew I'd be cared for when the time came for me to be cared for. That's what Rose didn't have, and that's what she was looking for, I felt, starting with that baby in her arms.

Then I realized that Mr. Giacomo didn't have the feeling of being welcome in our village either, though he and his wife have lived here for many years. It's hard to say how I knew this. There was a wary deference in the way people chatted with him in the street or in his café. Everyone called him Mr. Giacomo.

While Rose went into the lit-up station to buy tickets, my father carried her suitcases to the platform. I saw her under the yellow light of the station's tall windows, walking to the double doors that let out a vapour when they opened. I could hear the squeak of her suede boots in the new snow while she tried to walk in a normal, unaffected way. Carrying the newborn wrapped in a blanket, she stumbled once, tripped over her own feet.

My father gave me a twenty dollar bill. "Sweetheart, you look after her," he said. "Help her get settled." He wrote our phone number under the chin of the queen as if he thought that, once out of town, I'd never be able to remember it, then folded the bill twice before my eyes and drew my sleepy, half frozen fingers out of my coat sleeve to close them over the folded bill.

All the anger and fear that I'd seen in his eyes when he'd found Mr. Giacomo in our house had faded. "You're right to get away," he'd told Rose in the car. "Mr. Giacomo isn't one to give up. Stubborn as a mule in the beginning, but he spoils everything he touches." Then he asked me to go with her, to help her get settled.

Now he said, "Call me from Field." He was such a quiet man; usually he hardly said anything.

Soon after the Giacomo baby's death, my mother told me that she didn't know what to do with herself. All the joy had gone out of her work. Standing there on the platform, I felt her entire desolation. I understood then that trying to replace that lost baby with Rose's wouldn't heal my mother. I was torn between going with Rose or going home to her. You can never tell how much you really matter. The kind of difference you make.

My father, watching Rose return from the station, said, "You *have* to go with her." He must have sensed my hesitation.

Carrying that baby, she was hurrying, and she looked at the same time vulnerable and alone, determined and scared.

She took me by the hand down the train corridor. We climbed into a narrow bed behind heavy curtains. I raised the blind to the lit-up platform that was rolling past at a walk, the clacking of the wheels and she on her side. Rose combed her hair while the newborn nursed at her breast. She had a nightshirt for me in a marbled green suitcase, warm from the stove where it had hung drying. Lying beside her I touched the little hollows in the small of her back that were the colour of pips left on raspberry canes after you pick the fruit.

The bed was narrow, and I felt pushed against the metal wall. The heavy curtain smelled of rug cleaner. Rose's feet were icy cold on my ankles.

She said, "We're going," and I could sense her smile in the dark. She was going away to her new life, eighteen years old. People talk about responsibility, being mature, but they don't know what they're talking about. Mostly they mean, Do what I tell you. Outside I could see the dawn over the mountains through the flickering snow and when we went over the Palliser Bridge I saw my father's mill upriver on the bank, snow-covered ice in the shallows. "Your feet smell, Lacey," Rose said.

I saw that the toes of my socks were stained with blood and fluid. In the hurry to leave our house, I'd put on the shoes I'd had on when I'd pressed my knees into the small of Rose's back during the birth. Some of the blood must have seeped into them. I climbed out of bed to throw away my socks in the washroom, scrub my shoes in the sink with hand soap. I couldn't scrub them hard enough to get that smell off. I hooked one foot then another in the sink, scrubbing at my feet and between my toes with a facecloth till they were red.

When I returned to the train bed, Rose handed me her baby and said, "Walk him a bit for me, won't you? I need to sleep."

That child hardly weighed more than the winter blanket I wrapped him in, and I felt his toes wriggling. I was worried that he might wake up and that I wouldn't know what to do. So I kept walking, afraid that he would cry.

We were standing on the metal plates between cars and I was watching the mountains through a window opening that had no glass in it. Snow hissed over the face of the mountain. We were slowly climbing out of the valley and I drew the blanket loosely over Senna's face to keep him warm.

In the train bed she'd told me she'd decided to call him Senna.

I felt afraid without knowing why. In the village museum there are school photos from the 1920s: dirty-haired boys with wide, still eyes and girls with prim smiles, all out there in their faces — *they* had gone on to work in the sawmill or drugstore, marriage, the house on 4th Street, the kids, a trip to Scotland or Italy, piling up experiences like money deposited in a bank. Then a car accident or a heart attack, a funeral and a mossy stone, mostly the usual thing. It all made me feel so tired. But maybe

a class photo, a bit of a second, was more than
enough in any life, if you just paid attention to
what you already have in your arms.

In the winter of 1964, when I was eleven, I
sneaked out at night to go ice fishing on Olebar
Lake. I took a flashlight and a yew wood reel. I had
a mason jar of crayfish in my coat pocket. It was
so cold that the ice hummed like a violin string
and stars glittered like a thousand miles of mica.
Alberto Braz had marked the hole he'd chopped
in the ice with a bundle of sticks tied with a ribbon
that shimmered in the starlight. It was a long way
out there and quiet and once I heard the huff of
a moose in the dark firs along the far point. No
one else on the lake that night, all the fishing huts
closed up. I cleared ice out of the hole with my bare
hands; I ran around in circles to attract fish by
underwater vibrations. I laid the flashlight down,
set my line, and soon I was hauling in trout after
trout, little things with a blue and green speckle on
their sides and the smell of archival water on them.
Soon I had a heaped pile at my side with the ones
on the outside beginning to freeze. Hungry, they
just kept taking the bait.

There was no one else out there to see how lucky I was that night.

I kept looking around for someone to see what was happening.

And then, all of a sudden, I saw myself and what I had at my feet: way too many, too quickly and without much effort. Looking at the poor little things, I felt my stomach turn. I cleared away the frozen ones, the light had already gone out of their eyes. Five or six in the middle of the stack were still alive. Heartsick, I let them go.

⊞

Now I heard the car door slide open and Rose was standing beside me. To stay awake, I'd rested my forehead against the metal wall. The wind in the window opening was numbing my ears. The forest ran by and the rock peaks above were just beginning to show. After a while she said, "Give me him, I can't sleep."

When she returned to the sleeping car, I felt the train slow between high, sooty banks. We were climbing into the mountains. I walked through the dining car past linen-covered tables with flower vases bracketed to the wall and on each a peach in a silver bowl. An unripe peach is hard and sounds like an empty wooden box. The skin of a ripe one bunches under your thumb. I was hungry and tucked one under my shirt.

Then, thinking of Rose, I felt she was in trouble.

I hurried, almost ran back to our sleeping car.

I was remembering how in the fall of '68, Mr. Giacomo had paid us to find his horses that had come down from the alpage. I remembered that in the Slocan Gorge we could smell their grassy breath: his two buckskin horses were on the path. I could hear the clop of iron shoes and the suck of heavy shoes in the mud. They were coming down slowly, unsure, because the Palliser Range was buried in snow. In those days Mr. Giacomo was a trail guide, and he often took them into the mountains. They were coming down to their winter stables in the first snow.

"Lacey," Rose said then, "it's Mr. Giacomo's horses."

To let them approach, we stood by the path under the pines. I felt a warm muzzle brush my shoulder and arm. On their breath I could smell the sweet range grass that crackled when you walked through it. I could hear snow melting in the bearded moss that hung from the pines. The air had turned warm and it smelled of rain. Suddenly the horses tore away.

The clouds we'd seen south of there had gathered overhead. Hailstones raked through the pines. Shadows rolled over the mountainside and the air, suddenly cold, smelled like breath out of a well. We heard splintering wood in the trees across the ridge, then thunder heaved the forest floor.

I ran into the forest to press my forehead against a pine trunk. Whimpering, I locked my arms around the tree. Rose unlaced my fingers one by one.

"Look at me," she said, backing down the path, gazing into my wild eyes and holding me steady in her gaze. My hands clutched hers like old roots.

And now on the train I felt the same way, and I went looking for her.

When I got to the observation car, I heard Rose talking. She was sitting on the carpeted platform under the glass dome at the rear. Until I was beside them, I couldn't see that it was Mr. Giacomo she was talking with. He was wearing his sheepskin coat and riding boots. He was in one of those tall, cloth-covered observation chairs, his hands clasped between his knees. He must have walked to the station to get on the train before we did.

"You belong at home," he told Rose, adding, "Honey, you're leaving a good place behind."

"You really don't care about us," Rose said.

"What will you do away, in Field?"

"I'm going to work in a hotel." Rose looked at him defiantly.

"But who will look after your baby?"

Rose handed me the baby and unwrapped the cold omelet that she'd brought. She hurriedly and silently tore it to pieces to give me some. I could see her wrinkled brow and I saw her begin to hesitate.

So little warmth came through the blanket, it was almost like the baby wasn't there; a hand floated up to touch my cheek. He reminded me of an owl I'd found on the Palliser road, stunned by a car. I'd covered it with a beach towel to carry it to the gravel shoulder, wings tucked under my arm next to my rib cage so that it couldn't push them out. Though it was bigger than a cat, it weighed hardly anything, all feathers and hollow bones.

"We have to keep going," I told her. "It's what you wanted, remember?"

I could see that all her excitement at leaving for a new life was fading, worn away by her fear of being alone. There was a sudden desolation in her eyes. She was wrapping up the pieces of omelet that she'd left untouched, wrapping and unwrapping them as if not sure what to do with the food.

"Field is too far away, " Mr. Giacomo nodded, watching her fumbling hands and mocking her gently. "Farther than Mrs. Hiraki's."

I hated his know-it-all patience then. He was trying to turn her around, turn her around with his mild confidence, his answers for every problem that she might have.

He was telling her that she could have the apartment above the Giacomo café and that she could work for him there. "Just a few afternoons a week to get you settled, then we'll see from there. You can stay with us as long as you like. Lacey here can visit when she wants."

"But he can't have two mothers," Mr. Giacomo advised her. *"Don't take away his good fortune."*

He smiled and leaned in to touch my knee, as if to tell me that he was right or maybe to show that I agreed with him. I pulled away, shrank back in my seat.

"All right," I heard Rose say. "All right then. I can't do this on my own. I'm too scared."

"Thank you for helping me," she said to me. "Thank you! We're going back."

When I crawled under the blanket to hold Mrs. Giacomo after her baby died, I felt how icy cold she was, shivering, and now that cold grief flared through me.

Now, when anyone touches me, I pull away without thinking. Have you ever felt that way? It comes to me like a spark of static electricity, as when you barefoot it across a carpet on a dry morning and touch a door handle.

⊞

In the winter of '69, a few months after Rose met Michael Guzzo, I saw him in the Starlight Theatre.

In those days, my mother bought theatre tickets

so she could sleep in the theatre. We'd go up the side aisle to where there was hardly anyone and wrap ourselves in blankets. She said she slept best in places where sleep surprised her, in the depot waiting for the bus to Naramata, on trains or in farm trucks returning home after a birth, jarring down the valley roads with a towel bunched on the rocker panel for a pillow, sleeping while the sun climbed over Odin Mountain, a dusty, rosy light flaring over the windshield. She slept a dreamless sleep and she awoke reluctantly, touching her dry lips and rubbing her eyes, looking around in all innocence or startled by where she was. Till all the worries rushed in, she briefly looked young and she had all the mussy-haired sleepiness of a little girl. Then she'd remember the Giacomo baby's death, but there was a moment or two when she didn't remember and I imagine the world was as it was, the flare of light on the Illecillewaet snowfields through the truck window, the long face of Cary Grant on the screen, the Palliser Valley orchards spreading by the bus window, and she was momentarily okay.

One night we were sitting below the prow, a little raised platform in the theatre where the sawmill

crew usually sat. Michael Guzzo had come in. My
mother was asleep and I watched him take short
steps down the aisle, feeling his way in the blinding
screen light, turning to look over us. He smelled of
cedar sawdust, and the sawmill crew called out as
he went past,

Keep your head down, Guzzo, we can't see!

Where's Rose?

Is she here?

He raised an embarrassed hand to brush away
their laughter and to shield his eyes.

Yes, she was here somewhere.

They were showing *North by Northwest* and in the
light of Mount Rushmore's face and Cary Grant's
frantic running, I saw Rose reach up to take his
hand and I heard her whisper:

It's you!

She took his hand to draw him down, and he
put an arm around her to muss her hair.

I felt jealous then, watching how they sat so close
together, and I wondered whether a boy would ever
hold me like that.

How did he go from her life?

That winter he was only in town to earn money

to travel. His uncle, almost blind and no longer able to work, had bought an interest in the Odin Mill. They had hired him as a family obligation, though he turned out to be a good worker, reliable, and even when they were cutting edge grain cedar for the Vancouver boatyards, he showed up for work, forearms bandaged because the oil in the dust raised welts on his skin.

Rose told me that he'd left to travel in Central America before she even knew she was pregnant.

The mill was going to shut down because of the coming snows, and he couldn't see sitting out the winter idle. He promised her that he'd be back in the spring, when the boss said they'd be rehiring.

Why are you going, Rose had asked him. They were sitting together on the narrow, cushioned seat by the linoleum table in his trailer on the Palliser, and she'd drawn away to look at him carefully.

She could see that this wasn't the whole truth. There was a sadness in him that she couldn't touch or hold or lessen, and it confused her.

He told her that he'd been drifting since his family had lost their land, their village, that he couldn't find a place to settle down in.

But you are coming back?

Yes, he reassured her.

There was a lake in Central America he wanted to see, in a volcanic crater where the Maya said clouds were born. Once in the Grizzly Bookstore he'd shown me a photo of it: there was a lone fisherman on a shore of pumice stones; bundles of sticks with ribbons tied to them showed against the water, and the sides of the crater, covered in pines, rose steeply all around. He had found this photo in a book at the back of the store, among the secondhand volumes he called train books.

What's so special about a lake? I asked him.

He closed the book then, touched its cover, a childlike, fragile look in his eyes that I felt drawn to.

Who knows what I'll find there? he said with a smile.

A sacred lake that he wanted to see. Have you ever felt that, amazed at what people do? That the wanting was enough for him to go? What are "wants"? And do they really matter that much, "I want this" and "I want that" and therefore I shall go? Doesn't

it get a bit tiring after a while, wanting things?
Don't you get worn out? What if you didn't want
anything at all, what would happen to you then?

14

*This morning I weeded the herb beds, painted the outhouse.
I got a call from a lookout in the Asher Valley and went
out on the catwalk to watch a narrow, boiling mass of
clouds send bolts, some of them visible for seconds, into
the ridge at my feet. I could hear the electricity zinging*

around the aluminum eavestroughs, crackling and sparking. Curtains of virga swept across Leon Creek.

Because maybe the cabin would be hit by lightning I knelt trembling on a stool with glass insulators in the bottom of the legs. Helicopters were in the air to the south, tracking three fires that I'd spotted. Every time I finished taking a bearing from the fire finder I'd look up to see another tree explode into flames before I could finish filling out the last message.

Later this evening, the unmistakable smell of wood smoke. I sat up in bed to look north and made out in moonlight a column rising straight up, thick with burning fir or pine pitch.

Because it was night, no one could be flown in to that fire in the Bremmer Valley. The road in was switchbacks through canyons, so it would take three or four hours to drive to the scene. High, strong winds, I write in the log book.

In the Bremmer Valley, there's a wet hollow of alder saplings. I don't know how they got in there. The valley is narrow and dark and only gets a couple of afternoon hours of light. A raw wind must have carried in alder seeds, all at once, so that a field of them grew young and springy, their trunks no thicker than my thumb. Someone had tried to farm in there once, leaving only a fence line of rotten cedar posts grassed over, a scattering of lichen-covered apple trees that looked crouched and huddled in themselves, like cats moved into a new house, and a hollow for a root cellar.

A few weeks before Senna was born, I walked from the fire tower to the Bremmer Valley, to lay out an armful of alder saplings to dry in the field among the apple trees, shaking the soppy earth that was full of shale from their roots. A week later I took in a saw to cut off the root balls and I stripped the canes of withered leaves, carried them back to the cabin to weave into a crib. I wasn't sure it would ever be used but I wanted it just in case Rose needed me to take him. I'd offered to help her and I wanted to be sure I could. I laid in towels for bedding in a frilled pillowcase and tied to the side a mobile of painted pinecones that I knew would make her laugh, so that he'd have something to look at. I even made rockers out of bent saplings tied with fishing line and I placed it under the north window and moved my little collection of books to the east sill. Those were warm days, maybe the last of the season, and the fireweed was in second bloom along the Palliser Ridge. When I sat out on the catwalk for hours, it felt like midsummer and I could smell the heat in the cedar siding, waiting.

Whole days and nights went by, billowed in time, and I didn't know what was happening to her.

Now I see headlights on the dust roads, crews driving in to take out weekend campers and river runners. By now the fire is in the pine and fir, trees torching off like matchsticks on the slopes of Bremmer Mountain. Burning debris tumbles and ignites more fires across the Palliser Ridge.

Later this morning a cold front is supposed to move in, bringing sleet and rain.

15

When I had a few days off, a month or so after we returned on the train, I went down from the fire tower to see Rose in her new apartment and to serve at the parish supper. It was hard to see her, after her decision to return. She always looked tired, as if she wasn't sleeping well, worn and quiet.

Though she had her own place now, though she was still in our village, every day she grew more distant, more unreachable.

Yet when I asked her how she was, she'd say, Fine! and look at me defiantly.

It grieved me to be around her. All the light-heartedness had gone out of her step; she no longer laughed in that quick, bright way that made you feel good. Another time when I was in town I didn't even go see her. I told myself I was too busy.

⊞

On the first morning of preparations for the parish supper, I got up early because my mother was up: I could hear her in the kitchen. She was making toast and coffee though it was still dark outside and the birds were asleep. She was dressed as I've never seen her before, in loose, light blue cotton slacks and a plain blue blouse. She looked younger.

"Where are you going?" I asked, wondering at the brightness in her eyes. All the worry had gone from her face. Though she was no longer dressed as a midwife, I asked, half-asleep, confused, "Is someone having a baby?"

I looked around for her midwife's bag that she usually put on the kitchen table to check through before leaving.

"I've given that up," she said. "I've another job." And in my astonished silence, she added, "Cleaning rooms in the Mackenzie Hotel."

I'd never seen her smile like that. She looked wide-awake, as if she'd just come from a swim in the lake. She was making herself a bag lunch, slicing bread and laying lettuce and sliced tomatoes and shredded ham on it, her hands light and quick. She took a couple of apples out of the refrigerator and a handful of raisins. These she put in a paper bag and she took a thermos of tea.

In her old job, she never had time to make food to take with her. When the call came, she would just get up, check the contents of her bag and go. Usually the family would feed her. Now she had time to sit and drink coffee before she went to work. She got up early, to sit at the kitchen table and listen to the awakening birds. Sometimes, she told me, she even read a newspaper or listened to the radio. There was no hurry, no emergency.

She called her new job — cleaning toilets, she

said: "I clean toilets in the Mackenzie Hotel"— the work of nonemergencies. She had no disasters to anticipate. No one was turning to her, full of pain, with a look that said, You're the only one here who knows what to do. Do something.

Lunch bag in hand, she said Mr. Giacomo had called to ask me to meet him by the river.

"He wants you to show him where to fish," she said. "For the parish supper."

⊞

On the Palliser banks, he asked me, "Do you think we'll have any luck?"

I said I didn't know.

We left the shore in his boat. I knew the deep pools under the bridge, where the sturgeon sleep like old dogs.

I remembered how he'd tried to touch my knee on the train and how my body had drawn away from him without even thinking. I didn't feel that I was myself around him anymore. It slowly settled in me that I was afraid of him. His smile was calm and inviting, the friendliest thing about him, but it made me afraid.

The metal line he let out had thread woven over it the colour of the shadows that flowed along the river bottom. The tip of his fishing rod was as thick as his thumb. The river was littered with alder leaves, so many coloured with a blue bloom, like ripe plums.

I counted eight boats on the sturgeon pool under the bridge. Every year at this time the village fished the river. By agreement only one sturgeon was taken, and it was offered to the priest.

"Since the death of our boy," he said, "my wife and me are like old people." He laughed. "We must look like we're cut out of cardboard! I believe people here see us that way," touching the corners of his eyes. When he looked at me his eyes were full of shame.

"Mrs. Giacomo hasn't left her room for weeks. Do you think Rose is going to keep her child? It must be so hard for her."

His face showed the same quiet patience that I'd seen on the train.

The sky had settled over the river and already a few flakes were falling; almost like night the way the light had faded, the snow beginning to cling to the sandbar. The jacket he handed me smelled of wood smoke, of the campfires the village had lit on the sandbar while we fished for the new priest and of the gasoline he'd poured into the outboard motor tank. He draped the jacket over my knees with raw hands touched by the cold, his knuckles swollen. He was massaging his knuckles and I wanted to give him my mitts but he said no, he was fine.

"Of course she's going to keep the baby," I said then. I'd put on a look of complete confidence. "Your helping her isn't going to make any difference."

For a while he looked at me quietly. "Well that's it, then," he said. "I guess there's nothing more I can do."

He looked at me again and in his eyes there were still flashes of hope. "Rose has changed her mind before," he said. "Maybe she'll change it again."

In the stern at his feet there were paper lanterns with cutouts pasted to them: horses and stars, half-moons, birds. Those were lanterns for the parish supper. Mr. Giacomo had brought them along for me to repair. I reglued the curled arms of foil stars, horses' heads, crumpled birds' wings that the Grade Twos had made from construction paper, fingertips numb in the river wind that came up in the morning.

He asked me if we should pull up our lines to try another pool, but I didn't know for sure, and briefly his face looked sad. He couldn't fish in one place for fear the fish might be caught in another. I really don't know the river that well: a lot of easy and broken water, light and dark places.

He touched the corners of his eyes. His face was almost grey in the cold mist rising from the river.

I thought about what he'd said: about how he thought people in the village saw him and his wife in their grief. Like old, used-up people, he'd said, like cardboard cutouts. And he wanted a place of honour in our village. He'd always wanted to be among the best people, to fit in that way. Yet his wealth had not been enough to guarantee the health of his family, the respect of our village.

"I'm sorry," I said to him then. "It can't be helped."

It was not Mr. Giacomo's boat that caught the priest's fish. Mr. Beruski caught it. Early afternoon, by way of a gaff-hook in its jaw, Mr. Beruski pulled the sturgeon onto the sandbar. It was lying on its side, gasping, and I covered its black eye with my hand.

"Over one hundred pounds," said Mr. Giacomo. He walked its length, prodding its belly full of roe, a disappointed look on his face.

Sometimes I look for a change in my luck too. The morning before I came down from the fire tower, I saw three crows fly by the north window, each making the point of a triangle and I said to myself that's a sign things are going to get better for my friend Rose. I was that desperate for encouragement.

Later that afternoon, pulling handfuls of soppy rotten leaves from the rain gutters on our house, I saw my mother hurry across the street. She'd been working at the hotel, lost track of time, and wanted to be home waiting for my father who was down at his one vat mill. On the ladder I saw what she hadn't noticed — that he, too, was in the street. He had stepped behind a transport truck so that she wouldn't see him under the street light that had just come on. This was a new game that they played, the waiting for each other. For the pleasure of seeing you. If she had slipped and fallen in the icy street he would have run to her. Her new life of nonemergencies was making her happy again, and so he was happy.

16

Four men carried the fish to the priest. With the
sturgeon wrapped in a black tarp, they stood at
the church doors. They had brought it up a river
path, then along 3rd Street to the church. Although
Mr. Giacomo was at the head walking with Rose

in her waitress outfit, the others did not allow him to carry any of the weight. He might as well have been carrying air. He pretended for the onlookers, but his arms were slack. I saw this, standing on the corner of 3rd Street and Columbia Avenue.

In our village, when people make up their mind that you're generally more trouble than you're worth, the hints at first are often subtle. There was this drifter who took a job on the green chain at the Odin Mill. Things started to go missing: gloves, work boots, a sandwich from a lunchpail. One day he sat down at the lunch table to pour tea from his thermos. He filled his cup with bunker oil. No one said anything, the whole crew was there at the lunch table, watching. He quit within the week, took his pay and left.

People could see what was happening with Rose, I wasn't the only one. People could see how worn and tired she'd become, that a wall had been put up around her.

⊞

Earlier, in her room above the café, I'd brought Rose the rust-coloured paper raincoat I'd found in the

Grizzly Bookstore. I told her that the procession was about to start and that Mr. Giacomo was waiting for her by the river. I said she could wear the paper raincoat in the procession. On an unpainted wooden table there were roadside cornflowers in a slender vase, their leaves curled and withered. She had changed into her waitress clothes to go to work in the Giacomo café and was combing out her hair that clung to the brush with static.

Along the sill, light played on small pieces of driftwood she'd collected. On one she'd painted, bright blue, the eye of a fish because it looked like a fish and on another she'd painted a horse's mane. She'd sanded the pieces and polished them with beeswax. Light spilled over them as the shine spilled on her combed hair. After I picked one up, my hand smelled faintly of honey.

She said, "Early in the morning before shift we go along the river to find new pieces he can play with. I like to make my own things for him."

"I couldn't see myself in Field," she said. "I felt scared thinking about it. Mr. Giacomo is nice enough, as long as I go along with what he says. If I don't he gets mad."

She had no dresser, so her clothes were carefully folded in the two open suitcases she had taken on the train to Field. The baby's clothes were stored in bins under the secondhand crib my mother had bought for her, and he was asleep in there. Because the apartment was above the café, she only had to walk downstairs to work, and she would call the bar telephone and leave hers off the hook so that she could hear his cries should he awake while she was working. She hadn't put up curtains because she didn't know how long she would be there. After shift she'd carry up a plate of leftovers to make baby food — whirred squash or peas and pabulum — in a blender that she'd take apart and leave to clean in the sink. There was no music or radio and all you could hear was the traffic in Columbia Avenue or the crackle of the frost melting on the east windows when the sun came up over the alley at midmorning; she had a towel bunched there to collect the dripping water.

The place filled me with silence, the silence of waiting and of being unsure of yourself. It made me feel quiet and expectant and I didn't know what I was waiting for. Even the creak of the floorboards sounded loud and edgy, maybe because there was hardly any furniture and the echoing ceiling sloped on two sides to join the walls at shoulder height.

I'd bought the paper raincoat for her, thinking she'd like to wear it, but she laughed and said no, turning down my gift.

She held the raincoat up to herself to check the fit; it had the luminescence of corn snow. It had been waterproofed with persimmon tannin.

"No," she said again, stroking out a sleeve to flatten it along her arm. "Honey I don't think so. Mr. Giacomo won't like it. He wants me to show up in my waitress things, to represent the café."

"Why don't *you* wear it?" she asked.

I thought that she would have been bold enough to wear it in the procession, to stand up to him, but I was wrong. Her laughter had sounded sharp and false.

"Do you like this place?" I asked her.

Now she looked at me thoughtfully. She picked up her brush and wrinkled her brow.

"You're my friend, right?"

"Yes, Rose," I nodded.

"No, I don't like this place. It doesn't feel right."

"Why not?"

"It doesn't feel like my home. I always feel we're being watched. I can't go anywhere without Mr. Giacomo asking, Where are you going? When will you be back? I try to pretend that we're okay but we're not."

At that moment she had lost her defiant, determined look. It no longer felt like she was pushing me away, and I could see how lonely and vulnerable she had become. I felt then that I could help her, and a memory came to me.

"Do you remember the night we went wading in the lake in the snow, when that house came out of the mist?"

She nodded, smiling.

"And Mr. Giacomo in the window?"

"Yes."

"Do you remember how anxious and worried he sounded when he called out to us, Who's there? Can't you hear Mr. Giacomo saying to your boy, 'Where are you going? When will you be back?' while he grows up in that Burton house? And where will *you* be?"

"Why is he that way?"

"I don't know," I said. "I feel he's always trying to hide something."

She was sitting at the table by the window, the hairbrush in her hand. I bent down and gave her a kiss.

17

Each year I have to climb farther, a little farther, a few hundred yards or so, to bury my father's paper in the snowfields. Everywhere there is reflected light.

The morning of the parish supper, before I loaded the truck to drive up to the snowfields, my father laid out a two-by-three-foot sheet on his work table. You could see the impression of the grain of the yew wood drying board on it, under a powder snow luster. It smelled like straw.

Lacey, he said to me, running his hand over it, not one flaw, not one impurity. It's like a new human soul.

I drove up to the snowfields to lay out the paper and cover it with snow. Those sheets were translucent and they had a fine satiny sheen. Because of their purity, they'd last maybe hundreds of years. They were so strong you could pass them through a finger ring and they wouldn't shred.

They would outlast me.

I thought of all those trout I caught when I was ten years old. I knew the ones on the outside of the pile were already dead: all the light had gone out of their eyes. No light, no life.

When I got back to town, I went to look for Rose in the Giacomo café. She was disinfecting the kitchen counter where the fish would be prepared; her hands and arms, flushed to the elbows, smelled of bleach. Mr. Giacomo asked me to help him carry glass panes and the winter door up from the café cellar. We unhinged the sidewalk shutters, unscrewed the hinges from the cedar sash and fitted in winter storm panes and the pine wood door. Watching us, some passersby stood for a moment under the awning, under a darkening sky.

All the storefronts were lit up and the sky had turned a dark grey. Trees on the mountain stirred. In the café washroom, I folded and rolled an evening's fresh towels and placed them in the v-shaped rack by the sink.

When I came into the dining room, Rose was standing by the bar.

"I'm going back to the Big Bend to live with my parents," she announced.

"Oh, you'll not be leaving," Mr. Giacomo said and he touched her ducked head, laughing and smiling at me. "This is where you belong."

I couldn't imagine Mr. Giacomo touching me like that; it just seemed impossible that you'd allow him to touch you.

All of a sudden I felt very tired, and I went to sit in a chair by the window. It smelled of varnish because Mr. Giacomo had varnished the sill. I was wearing a loose-knit sweater that I'd bought in the Grizzly Bookstore. It felt like the weight of an extra blanket, because in one pocket there was a folded page torn from a book and in the other a Japanese bowl.

Rose came up behind me, to drape her arms over my shoulders. I couldn't see her eyes and I couldn't imagine the expression in them. I could feel the light weight of her forearms on my shoulders, the stillness of her gaze. I could see the freckles on the back of her hands and on her wrists that smelled of bleach. Under her resting arms I felt like a bundle of tense sticks.

To free myself, I leaned forward to rest my fingertips on the sill. The varnish gripped my fingertips when I touched it, like frost on a metal door handle.

I went over to Mr. Giacomo's table, and I laid out before him the book page from my pocket and the Japanese bowl. He stared at them, and then at me.

I should say how I got that bowl.

I'd heard that work had stopped on the Burton house, and I went there that afternoon to see Mrs. Giacomo. I'd been wondering how she was. I'd brought a book with me that I wanted to show her. It's called *A Catalogue of Unrecovered Items, Volume Four: Pottery and Clay Figurines*, a train book that Michael Guzzo had bought in the Grizzly Bookstore. It was published by the Allied Powers after the war. In the introduction it says that the catalogued items, some of them identified by insurance photographs, were never recovered during the occupation of Japan, and the purpose of the catalogue, in several volumes, was to pass on the work of recovery to future generations.

The kitchen was still filled with unpacked boxes, the green cushion from the sofa in the downstairs hallway was still on her bed. I could hear the garden hose dripping in the kitchen sink. I ran my hand along the plaster walls, smooth as a yew wood drying board. They gave off a soft glow and they smelled like chalk. There were footprints up and down the hallway in the plaster dust, some of them my own. The propane heaters stood collected at the doorway. The camp stove still had a pot on it, a thin skin of dust on the bottom of the pot. The two clay bowls that Mr. Giacomo wanted to drink from in celebration were still on the counter. I leafed through the book, found the photo I was looking for. Those bowls were from the Tokugawa period, just as Mr. Giacomo had said, the potter's mark incised in the base. His wealth hadn't come from logging in the Nachako country. His wealth had come from artifacts he'd stolen at the end of the war. He had worked as a translator on Shido Island and used his knowledge to profit from the war.

I hated him then. I hated his lies, the sham way he'd gone about making a place for himself in our life. I hated him and Mrs. Giacomo, too, for the way they were trying to wall Rose in with their grief.

I pocketed one of those bowls. I stayed for an hour or so, lit candles that sputtered and crackled. I looked through Mrs. Giacomo's dresser drawers for her clothes and I looked under the foyer bench for any sign of recently worn shoes. I found out later she had left, maybe soon after the birth, moved back to their house on 4th Street, where she stayed alone in her room.

Now I placed the bowl very tenderly, gently before him, quietly, like in the stillness when the hawk comes. I smoothed out the page with the photograph on it as though it were a precious sheet, pure washi. I felt that something inside me was just about to break.

I didn't want him to have the whole book, just

that page. Maybe he had other things that were in that book. But I only knew about the bowls, so that was all I could accuse him of.

The crinkles at his eyes deepened and paled, but he smiled.

"So you know," he said, and I nodded.

"They had lost the war," he smiled, "the ones we interrogated. The crown prince, the naval officers. We only took from them what they'd already stolen during their retreat."

He paused, and a shadow drew into his eyes.

"That happened so long ago," he said, a softness in his voice. "It's not something I think about often."

I started yelling at him then. I told him not to waste his confident smile on me. It might look like he was trying to help Rose, but he was just hemming her in with his deceit. And nothing he had to offer was worth one touch of her freckled hands, one moment of her dancer's grace.

Just then Rose came out of the kitchen. "What's going on?" she asked.

"Nothing!" and he quickly balled up the sheet and pocketed it, put the bowl on a glass shelf behind the bar, by the upturned wineglasses.

That was the last time I spoke to Mr. Giacomo.

I left, didn't stay for the parish supper. I was shaking, exhausted, and yet I felt a kind of joy. I walked down our main street towards the tracks, hating his complacent smile, hating the fact that he didn't seem to care about what I felt. He was going to have his family his own way, at whatever the cost. But I wasn't going to let him.

What if Michael Guzzo found out that he was a father? With all the loss that he'd had in his life, maybe this was one loss he wouldn't allow to happen, pushed out of the life of his son. Maybe it would be important for him to say to the Giacomos, Enough, this you can't take from me.

18

Yesterday, when I got back to the fire tower from my days
off, I brought along the ticket I'd bought to Guatemala City.
I knew that Michael Guzzo was somewhere in Guatemala.
The photo that he'd shown me was of a sacred lake in the
district of Quetzaltenango, in the western highlands of that
country. I'd decided to go find him.

As soon as I got in the door I saw that the cabin was not as I'd left it: my bed had been pushed to the north wall, the chrome-legged chairs had been moved from the east to the west window, my basil plants shuffled along the banister, the cutlery switched in the hutch, the stacked dishes pushed back on the counter. Nothing was where it was and I felt terrified, as if this place were not mine, as if I'd lost my life.

One book was missing from my collection on the east sill, the *Catalogue of Unrecovered Items*.

Just at dawn, the sound of dripping water. Everywhere I could hear melting snow. Today the cabin is to be boarded up for the winter, plywood nailed over glass, the doors locked. Through the window by my bed, I see snow water flowing over frost on a rock outcrop that looks like strands of a girl's hair. Lightning storms that used to sweep through this valley go on the other side of the foothills. Now I see smoke from campfires on Olebar Lake.

Below, in the village, people are turning on their breakfast lights.

The logging fires are still smouldering on the Palliser Ridge, a white, drifting smoke that reminds me of washi paper.

When I applied for this job, the Forestry Service questioned my young age, my ability to be alone. That age and loneliness go together is not questioned.

When I was younger, I was more sure of myself, and now I feel porous, less contained, like a sheet of my father's washi. I go out of here in dreams and when I nod off I sometimes can't tell the difference between dream and memory and when I awake I look on myself as a stranger.

There is a squirrel sleeping in the wall; during the day it raids the bird feeders.

The pines below the ridge are singing. I can smell the resin in the swaying trunks. Last night's stars have a scoured midwinter sharpness. Outside the west window, one last star shows its grape petal rays.

There really are so many ways to be a little more gentle in this world.

Acknowledgements

EXCERPTS FROM THIS NOVEL HAVE BEEN PREVIOUSLY PUBLISHED IN
Writing Beyond History (MONTREAL: CUSMANO COMMUNICATIONS,
2006) AND AS A CHAPBOOK ENTITLED *Mio Zio* (TORONTO:
FLAT SINGLES PRESS, 1999).

FOR THEIR ENDURING SUPPORT AND FRIENDSHIP, MANY THANKS
TO ANNA, DEANE, REBEKAH, LAURIE, DREW, CHERYL, DAVE,
CHRISTIE AND FLOYD. THANKS ALSO TO MARILYN BOWERING,
STEVEN GALLOWAY, EDNA ALFORD, MARY WOOD, AND ESPECIALLY
TO PAUL MATWYCHUK, ANDREW WILMOT AND NATALIE OLSEN
AT NEWEST PRESS.

THE AUTHOR EXPRESSES HIS DEEPEST GRATITUDE TO TOM
WHARTON, EDITOR AT NEWEST, FOR HIS CAREFUL READING
OF THE ORIGINAL MANUSCRIPT AND FOR HIS ENTHUSIASTIC
SUPPORT OF *The Wheel Keeper* PROJECT.

THANKS ALSO TO VANCOUVER ISLAND UNIVERSITY AND TO
THE BANFF CENTRE'S WRITING STUDIO FOR THE TIME AND PLACE
TO COMPLETE AN EARLY DRAFT OF THE MANUSCRIPT.

ROBERT PEPPER-SMITH LIVES ON A FARM IN THE CINNABAR
VALLEY WITH HIS LOVE ANNA AND TEACHES PHILOSOPHY
AT VANCOUVER ISLAND UNIVERSITY. HE IS AT WORK ON THE
THIRD NOVEL IN THE WHEEL KEEPER SERIES, TENTATIVELY
ENTITLED *Lake of Memory.*

❡ THIS BOOK WAS TYPESET IN CENTAUR, RELEASED BY MONOTYPE.
THE ENDSHEETS ARE PRINTED ON DOMTAR COLORS 20-LB CHAMOIS.
THE TEXT PAPER IS 55-LB ROLLAND ENVIRO 100 NATURAL.

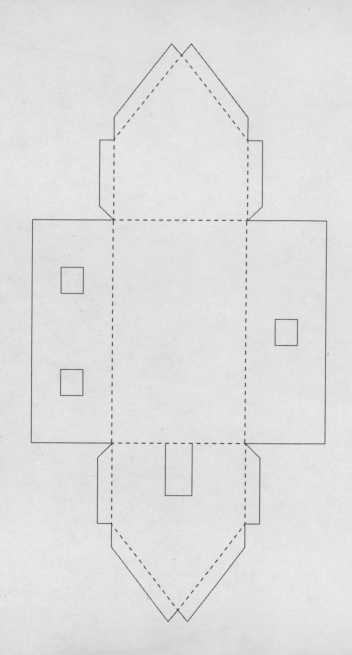